Dreamlandia

by Octavio Solis

A SAMUEL FRENCH ACTING EDITION

SAMUEL FRENCH

FOUNDED 1830

NEW YORK HOLLYWOOD LONDON TORONTO

SAMUELFRENCH.COM

ISBN 978-0-573-69799-9   Printed in U.S.A.   #29258

MUSIC USE NOTE

IMPORTANT BILLING AND CREDIT REQUIREMENTS

DREAMLANDIA was commissioned and produced by Dallas Theatre Center (Richard Hamburger, artistic director) on May 16, 2000. The performance was directed by Richard Hamburger and the assistant director was Marisela Barrere, with sets by Russell Parkman, costumes by Claudia Stevens, lighting design by Steve Woods, and music/sound design by Marty Desjardins. The production stage manager was Christy Weikel. The cast was as follows:

BLANCA	Zabryne Guevara
LAZARO	Carlo Alban
PEPÍN	Felix Solis
CELESTINO	Gino Silva
SONIA	Maggie Palomo
FRANK	Bernie Sheredy
DOLORES	Dolores Godinez
SETH	Scott Phillips
CARL	T.A. Taylor
BUSTAMANTE	Dolores Godinez
VIVIAN	Maggie Palomo

The West coast premiere of *DREAMLANDIA* was produced by, Dallas Theatre Center (Richard Hamburger, artistic director) at the Thick House in San Francisco, California. The performance was directed by Octavio Solis and the assistant director was Karen Macklin, with sets by Richard Olmstead, costumes by Karen Elsa Lee, lighting design by Rick Martin, and music/sound design by David Molina. The master electrician was Sophia Fong, the fight choreographer was L. Peter Callender, and the production stage manager was Amy Louison. The cast was as follows:

BLANCA	Dena Martinez
LAZARO	Sean San Jose
PEPÍN	Jorge Rubio
CELESTINO	Carlos Baron
SONIA	Carmen Elena Sosa
FRANK	Cully Fredricksen
DOLORES	Tessa Koning Martinez
SETH	Jonathan Kluger
CARL	Hank DiGiovanni
BUSTAMANTE	Tessa Koning Martinez
VIVIAN	Carmen Elena Sosa

CHARACTERS

BLANCA (ALFONSO) – Young woman
LAZARO – Young man
PEPÍN – Blanca's brother
CELESTINO – The Father
SONIA – His mistress
FRANK – Border Patrol Sector Chief
DOLORES – Dead, a ghost, Blanca's mother
SETH – Border Patrolman
CARL – Border Patrolman
BUSTAMANTE – played by **DOLORES**
VIVIAN – **CELESTINO**'s wife, played by **SONIA**

AUTHOR'S NOTES

The snatches of lyrics sung in Spanish are from "*Amor Eterno*"
by Rocio Durcal.

ACT ONE

PEPÍN. A night big as the state of Tejas with Pepín inside.

*(Pounding rain, punctured by lightning. Howitzer thunder. **VIVIAN** on a bed, screeching in pain. **PEPÍN** on floor by the bed, an open suitcase at his feet.)*

VIVIAN. *OH GOD* this *thing* eating me eating me eating me whole CELESTINO!

*(**CELESTINO** rips through the storm dragging **DOLORES** after him. **PEPÍN** rushes to her side. **FRANK** enters behind them and remains at a distance.)*

CELESTINO. There! Hurry! She needs you! *¡Ayudala!*

DOLORES. *Señor,* what can I do? *No se –*

CELESTINO. *Partera,* they call you! *¿Eres Partera?*

DOLORES. *Si pero –*

CELESTINO. Deliver this baby! Save my wife! Do it!

VIVIAN. Burning! My insides all black!

FRANK. Do it!

DOLORES. She belongs in a hospital! *¡Mira, sangre!*

PEPÍN. Mami, I wanna go home!

CELESTINO. I can't take her to a hospital! No-one can know! No-one can know anything!

DOLORES. I can't help her, *señor! ¡Tiene el Mal de Ojo!*

CELESTINO. *¡Mira!* I'll get you papers, a passport, I'll make you legal!!

DOLORES. *¿Papeles?*

CELESTINO. Everything! Just deliver my baby!

FRANK. He means it!

DOLORES. My cords, in the case! *¡Pepín, espera afuera!*

VIVIAN. Pain filling me with flies, millions of flies.

PEPÍN. Mami pries the legs apart like a curtain.

VIVIAN. My breath become smoke.

PEPÍN. Mami thrusting hands inside the mulch of blood and birth.

VIVIAN. AYY!

DOLORES. *¡No quiere salir!* The wretch is afraid of the light!

CELESTINO. Soon, *mi amor! ¡Ya mero!*

VIVIAN. OH GOD!

FRANK. Don't speak! Don't try to move!…

PEPÍN. Rope in her fists, rope around his little crown, pull against the neverlife, pull against blood, Mami pulls, her veins thicker than lightning, thunder in her throat, pulling –

DOLORES. Come! –

VIVIAN. *Bastards!* –

CELESTINO. Wait! You're hurting her! STOP!

PEPÍN. A whole mess of *tripas*, intestines roping the bed, dragging him back and then Mami says…

DOLORES. *¡TENGO QUE ABRIRLA!*

(**FRANK** *slaps* **DOLORES** *his knife. The* **VIVIAN** *screams as an infant wails.* **DOLORES** *hoists the wet child.*)

FRANK. OH SWEET JESUS!

PEPÍN. Hanging like meat, a bald pale pigbody limp and dripping with *mamasangre*.

(*Lightning, then black, then a riverside. Rain swells the raging current.* **DOLORES**, **PEPÍN** *and* **CELESTINO** *with a gun.*)

CELESTINO. My beloved. My Vivian.

PEPÍN. Right on the lip of *Señor Grande*, his black tongue licking our shoes.

DOLORES. She was too sick. The cocaine made her slack.

CELESTINO. So much blood in a woman, who knew?

PEPÍN. River and night become one.

DOLORES. I did all I could, *señor*.

CELESTINO. Swim.

DOLORES. ¿*Como*?

CELESTINO. Both of you, in the water.

DOLORES. I don't understand. You told me I would get papers.

CELESTINO. You killed my wife. For that, you want citizenship? Swim back to Mexico, *bruja*!

PEPÍN. ¡Mami!

DOLORES. Please! Not my boy! He'll drown!

CELESTINO. Go!

DOLORES. I delivered your son! I saved him!

CELESTINO. Keep walking!

(**DOLORES** *and* **PEPÍN** *step into the rivertide.*)

DOLORES. *¡Celestino Robles, hombre desgraciado! ¡Ingrato!* I curse you, I throw my scorpion signs at you, liar, mojado, yes, I know, *mojado* like all of us, I spit ash and gravel on your name, I swear the boy by the stars will be raped, by the stars will he beget his rage, to shit blood on your affairs, poison the kiss of your woman, betray your own word, and love another man better than he ever loves you! *¡Te lo juro, demonio! Te lo juro!*

CELESTINO. SWIM, BITCH!

DOLORES. ¡SINCERO! ¡SINCERO! ¡DONDE ESTAS! ¡SINCERO!

(*Blackout.* **CELESTINO** *and* **PEPÍN** *wake from the same dream twenty years later, on separate shores of the river.*)

CELESTINO. Is that all it was? A dream?

PEPÍN. *Sueños sueños son.*

(**FRANK** *walks on.*)

FRANK. You know, cowboy, if I had a fifth of pity, I sure wouldn't waste it on you.

CELESTINO. I don't want your pity. I want your allegiance.

FRANK. Well, I am your dog, sir.

CELESTINO. I would've cut you loose years ago, Frank. I would've spared us both the obligation that keeps us eating off each other's plate.

FRANK. And I woulda thanked you. But I reckon misery loves Mexicans.

CELESTINO. Maybe so. But I'm not a Mexican.

FRANK. Right. So what was it this time? What sick little peach pip a conscience set you on this midnight dosey-doh?

CELESTINO. Vivian.

FRANK. I ain't hearing this.

CELESTINO. I saw her, Frank.

FRANK. I don't care.

CELESTINO. She was my wife!

FRANK. And my sister! Don't you forget that!

CELESTINO. Then why don't you dream her! Why doesn't the grief play over and over in your sleep? Why don't you hear the screams like I do?

FRANK. Maybe I got less to feel guilty about.

CELESTINO. It doesn't change the facts between us, brother.

FRANK. Only fact I live by is on that island out there.

(*Across the riverbank in Mexico,* **BLANCA** *drags with great heaving effort the drenched body of* **DOLORES.**)

CELESTINO. Listen!…

PEPÍN. *¿Mami?*

FRANK. I don't hear anything.

CELESTINO. It's not about hearing.

PEPÍN. Is Mamasangre drunk again?

BLANCA. I found her tangled in the rushes. Wrapped around an old tire.

CELESTINO. I think it's over, Frank.

BLANCA. *¿Como pasó, Pepín?* This morning when I went to work, she seemed fine. How did she end up in the river?

PEPÍN. She packed this case, and held me close to her liver which is brown like *cucarachas,* she said adios, said she was going back, said go to sleep, so I slept. Is she sleeping too?

CELESTINO. I think she's finally dead.

BLANCA. ¡AMA!

(She collapses in tears over her dead mother.)

CELESTINO. The bones are all played out. I waited my time and my time is done, *bruja.* I win!

FRANK. What are you on about?

CELESTINO. What the dream meant, Frank. It's over. The woman that cursed my life is dead. Do you know what that means?

FRANK. I'm a Baptist, Tino.

CELESTINO. Bring him, Frank. Bring my son.

FRANK. No and hell no. –

CELESTINO. It's time.

FRANK. Them's not the terms we struck.

CELESTINO. I decreed him to that hyphen between his mother's name and mine, right in the middle of the *Rio.* Now I decree my son home.

FRANK. He's not the son you think.

CELESTINO. He's a Robles and he belongs by his father.

FRANK. You don't know what being a father means.

(**FRANK** *goes.*)

BLANCA. Why did you do it, *Ama?* What in that damn country did you drown yourself for?

PEPÍN. She said she was going for *Sincero.*

BLANCA. My father?

PEPÍN. En *mis* dreams, I heard her calling for him while this big *chingon*, Mr. *Migra*, stood by the *Rio* like the sheriff of *pinchi* Walmart.

BLANCA. Sincero. That name *es mi destino*. Without *Ama*, what home, what country, do I live in? All the country I got left is Sincero.

(*pumping her mother's chest for air.*)

Let there be one *suspiro*, one breath in my mother's lung, one little pocket of *Bilis. Coraje. Susto!* Breathe into me your torment, Ama!

(**DOLORES** *emits a single gasp of air.* **BLANCA** *inhales it.*)

BLANCA. *(cont.) Asi. Asi.* In your trances, you always walked the water. Now it's our turn.

PEPÍN. Blanca...?

BLANCA. *Vamonos, Pepín.* Let's bury Ama and get going.

PEPÍN. *¿A donde?*

BLANCA. *Yankeelandia.*

(**BLANCA** *takes the suitcase and goes with* **PEPÍN**. **CELESTINO** *stands as lights change. The island...*)

CELESTINO. I feel you, boy, on the fringes of my sleep, hair parted, skin smooth and brown, little manicured fingers reaching for me, drawing me near, making me say...Lazaro.

(**LAZARO** *charges out from his lair screaming like an enraged animal until the heavy chain on his neck jerks him back.*)

If I could, I would've sucked you in and held you
till the right day the right moon the right sign and
then released you to your mother and let you be
the son you were supposed to be. But I couldn't
and she's gone and you're what family's left.

LAZARO. *¡Escuchame!*

(**CELESTINO** *goes.*)

Sombras. Shadows. Gassy dreamfuckers. As if *que si.*
As if *que no.* You know what rise they come from?
Your cuts and punctures. Ghosts slip out the seams
and walk. Cry for the homeblood. The wound is
mouth. The mouth has voice. Voice has blood.
Blood is home. Home bleeds Lazaro. And all the
time the voices are saying only no. *Cada vez que no.*
Every ever no. Never to be home. Never to see.
Never to feel. It makes *el pinchi* heart a gash. *Ay!*

(*He violently yanks at his chain.*)

Cadena. You one big motherfucking piece of jew-
elry. Hang on me, sister. Hang your shimmer on,
your metal *luz,* your clink and your clank and the
weight of that sound, hang your *pinchi* links on me
and let me show the world I may be screwed *pero,*
honey, I know how to accessorize!

O God, come to where the flavor is!

Gimme one day's good glossy full page dream *de*
liberty!

Let me stand in the ad *de mi* own manhood long
enough to feel *suave, y si no suave,* then *con puro*
attitude! How can you leave me like this, in my own
rags, with my body reeking me up *y mis* glossy girls
smiling in my face! How can you let them treat me
como un animal? I have seen Italian leather!

Es el mero skin of God.

LAZARO. *(cont.)* Black me out, *ese!* Just black me out! I got no place but this, I got no recall, no friend, *nomas el* Sugar Man *con los* cc's of T-rex *y mi* Happy Meal! I got no hope to hang on. Just fucking black me out, just –

(BLANCA rises out of the water like a vision. He hides.)

Whoa. *Ruquita.* Wass your game? What you play *en mi* sandbar? The dreamfuck sends me a cover girl. As if *que si.* Oh, *mira.* Her skin, not white but tinted-glass, full-page lips, the scent of Obsession in the *Vanity Fair,* issue 46, *pagina* 29, I be so good at these delusions.

(LAZARO steps out. They gape at each other in awe.)

Hey.

BLANCA. Hey. Listen. Have you seen this boy? I lost him in the current.

LAZARO. *Senorita* Godsend.

BLANCA. Did you see my brother come ashore here?

LAZARO. *Aqui.*

(LAZARO produces a small portable radio. He turns it on.)

BLANCA. What's your deal?

LAZARO. My deal? I live and he feeds me. I stay and he enlightens me.

BLANCA. What is this place? You live here? Smells like *mierda.*

LAZARO. My fully furnished hole. A water bowl and a dog dish. Every TV Guide *desde* 1976 *pero no* TV. I do the crosswords. What was Suzanne Somers' name on *Three's Company?*

BLANCA. Chrissie.

LAZARO. You *are* a godsend. *(the radio)* He needs batteries to live.

BLANCA. Duh..

LAZARO. I need pain.

(He shows her his arms, speckled with needle marks.)

BLANCA. Why are you *encadenado?*

LAZARO. For my own good. That's what *Tío* Sugar tells me. *Dice que* I'm a dangerous man. My knowledge of things can shatter the world to pieces. Do I look dangerous to you?

BLANCA. You look pathetic. My kid brother, he's dangerous. He once whacked off a cat's head with a hub cap. *Como el* Oddjob. SSSHHOOOO!

LAZARO. Laughing hurts my throat.

BLANCA. You gotta lose that chain, *ese.* This Uncle Sugar, he the one who put you here? Is he your *jefe?*

LAZARO. This chain is my *jefe.* My *mami* is the water all around. Can I touch you?

BLANCA. Uh-uh.

LAZARO. I won't hurt you.

(He slowly approaches her. Feels her skin.)

LAZARO. *(cont.) Que piel, que piel,* smooth receptive skin with a healthy glow. Enriched with moisturizing plant extracts. Velvety finish, rich and creamy for day-long comfort.

(her lips)

Safe and effective lip balm, imbued with rare florals for that treasured moment.

(her hair)

Ay, que maximum body and fullness. *Cada* follicle carefully revitalized for that healthy lustre and shine that nature gave you.

(He takes the ribbon from her hair and then smells her.)

A captivating signature fragrance, allergy-tested for all skin-types. I smelt you before.

BLANCA. You have?

(He retrieves from his hovel a stack of fashion maga-zines Elle, Vogue, Modern Woman, *etc. Sniffs earmarked pages.)*

LAZARO. Here. *(sniff)* Here. *(sniff)* You. *(sniff)* All of them you. But never dreamed you out. That took more T-rex than I could take. Who are you?

(noises off)

BLANCA. Not now. Wait, okay?

LAZARO. Where you going?

BLANCA. I have to go!

LAZARO. You can't leave like that! *Tienes que* set free me!

BLANCA. Look, I'll be right back.

LAZARO. FUCK NO! BITCH! You have to let me go! GET YOUR ASS BACK!

BLANCA. Brother, I'm gonna tell you once! You're gonna have to wait. I'll be back for you. I promise. *Te voy hacer* free.

(She goes.)

LAZARO. DREAMFUCKER!!!!

(He collapses in a heap, and rocks himself as he cries.)

Wish her back. Wish her back. Wish her back. See her. Wish her back. Squeeze her out again!

(He squeezes his needle marks. FRANK *and his two men enter.)*

FRANK. Hey, pilgrim.

LAZARO. *¿Eres tu?* Are you really there, Frank?

FRANK. Sure am. Look what I brung you. Claudia Schiffer in color. Beauty tips on Page 80. The new Fall Line.

LAZARO. mmgh.

FRANK. You don't sound too excited, son.

LAZARO. I don't need her no more, Frank. I seen the cover girl move.

FRANK. What cover girl?

LAZARO. I seen her shake her ass. She let me *tocarla*. Felt the ph balance of her skin. So rockin.

FRANK. Who are you talkin about? I didn't see no-one.

LAZARO. She's my ghost, Frank. She arose *de mis* sores.

FRANK. That can only mean one thing, son. It's time for you to check out.

LAZARO. *¿De veras?*

FRANK. Cmere, son.

(**LAZARO** *goes to him.* **FRANK** *gently holds him.*)

I know, boy. I know. Been a hell of a time for both of us. But I'm gonna free you. I'm gonna quit that pain and deliver you from the bonds of this world. Bring me that thermos.

(*They bring him the thermos. He opens it. Steam rises.*)

Fetch one of your cover girls, pilgrim.

(**LAZARO** *tears a page from a magazine and hands it to* **FRANK**.)

She's pretty.

(**FRANK** *tears the picture to little pieces and drops them in the thermos. Then he hands it to* **LAZARO**.)

FRANK. *(cont.)* Drink it all up.

(**LAZARO** *drinks.*)

LAZARO. It's strong.

FRANK. Brewed the way a special lady taught me. Now on your back. That's it, boy. Close your eyes.

(**FRANK** *unlocks the shackle from his neck.*)

LAZARO. I feel…like…kinda…free.

FRANK. That's darkness spreading you out.

LAZARO. Will I see cover girl there?

FRANK. Front row at the Latin Grammys. In a mink and black number slit up to here.

(**FRANK**'s *men slip a large sack over his head.*)

LAZARO. *Se siente* prickly. Does darkness feel so prickly?

FRANK. Darkness does, son.

LAZARO. I'm gonna find her, Frank. I'm gonna... hhh...

SETH. You don't have to do this, you know.

FRANK. Shut up, Seth.

SETH. Mr. Robles ain't the INS. You don't have to take orders from him.

FRANK. I said shut up. What the hell you know about this, dumbass?

SETH. Well, I know you like this kid more'n he does. –

FRANK. Dammit, Seth, this boy is an abomination to me. if it was up to me, he'd a been drowned long ago. It ain't up to me.

(**CARL** *finds the ribbon.*)

CARL. Lookit this, Frank. Where'd he get this?

FRANK. Maybe cover girl paid a visit after all. Put him on the boat. And you, mister, remember yourself. You gotta badge to uphold here.

(*They take up the sack and go.* **FRANK** *studies the ribbon.*)

FRANK. *(cont.)* Cover Girl? You mess with my pilgrim?

(**FRANK** *goes as* **PEPÍN** *enters, crying out after* **BLANCA**.)

PEPÍN. Blanca! ¡Blanca Dolorida! ¡Blanca de mi vida! Where are you?

(*He sees the audience.*)

Oofas! Who the refried beans are you! Are you…
waspichis? Ancient tribe of white people? Waspichis from the land of Wasp? *¡Chevre!* I thought
Americanos were taller, like that *presidente, como se
llama,* Rano…Rano…Rano Macdano! The big red
hair! Mami admire him so much, she dressed me
like him sometimes, put me on the street to do
presidential tricks. I juggle, I breathe kerosina and
vomit fire, make all the waspichi kiddies laugh.

Oofas, are you the *presidente? Orale,* presidunce, I
got one thing to say to you. these *problemas* with
the border that we got? I know how you can erase
them all, *mano!* Switch countries. That's right.
Move the US to the south and Mexico up north,
and watch how things change. Wait a minuto puto,
ain't that whass happening already? *¡Chale!* You're
a *chingon presidente!*

(**BLANCA** *appears behind him dressed in a man's
suit.*)

BLANCA. Pepín.

(*Startled,* **PEPÍN** *stands at attention and checks his
pockets.*)

PEPÍN. *Si señor.* I have *mis papeles.*

BLANCA. No, Pepín. It's me. Me.

PEPÍN. *¿Blanca? ¿Que te pasó, carnala?*

BLANCA. I'm a man now, okay? You gotta call me by my
man's name, okay?

PEPÍN. But where are your *chi-chis?*

BLANCA. As soon as I set foot in *Tejas,* my hair fell off
and I grew some things that I had to cover with
man clothes. Follow me so far?

PEPÍN. So we're in the Land of Billy Bob! Yeehaw!
Andale, Blanca's a cowboy! Yeeeehaw! Ride em,
pardner!

BLANCA. *Escucha*, Pepín. My name is Alfonso now. *No me llames* by that other name. No-one'll bother us if we're boys.

PEPÍN. Is the same thing gonna happen to me!? Can I have your *chi-chis*, please?

BLANCA. No, just me. I can't be a girl now. Not if I'm going to find him.

PEPÍN. Our father who art in Tejas?

BLANCA. Pepín, I want you to think. Does this look like the riverside in your dream? Are we close to that place?

PEPÍN. *¿Sabes que?* It's *un poquito* like it, but I think in my *sueño* it was this a-ways, gotta dream this a-ways, ooo-ooo-oooo!

*(He wanders off in a daze. **BLANCA** watches him.)*

BLANCA. *Pobre loquito.*

*(**DOLORES** appears as **PEPÍN** exits.)*

DOLORES. He was never meant to live.

BLANCA. *Ama.*

DOLORES. But he lives to spite us all.

BLANCA. *Ay, Ama. ¿Porque?* Why did you go in the river?

DOLORES. I had to, *mija.* Why did you bring Pepín? He's going to need a lot of care.

BLANCA. He's the only one who's ever seen him. He'll recognize him for me.

DOLORES. Your father.

BLANCA. You never showed us any pictures, you never told us anything but his name. A name you couldn't say without crying. In a house where from the ceiling hung all these herbs to dry and all these wooden *santos* stared out at me and the smells of healing filled my senses, there was no healing. This man caused you pain, Ama.

DOLORES. I had to die to stop it.

BLANCA. Now I got your pain. I have to stop it. Even if means coming to these *pinchis gringos*, I'll find him and I'll stop it.

DOLORES. Better make sure you got a green card, honey.

BLANCA. Is that all you have to say? Is that what you came for?

DOLORES. I came because I thought you were him. Those are his clothes you're wearing.

BLANCA. This…is his?

DOLORES. You stand like *Sincero* in those pants.

BLANCA. Oh god. They were in that old suitcase.

DOLORES. With those old records. Lucha Villa. Javier Solis. He loved those old Mexican boleros. *(sings)* "*Tu eres la tristeza de mis ojos que lloran en silencio por tu adiós…*"

BLANCA. I can't wear it…I can't…..

DOLORES. Wait, *mija*. Don't take it off. It does my swollen heart good to see his old coat filled with life again. You bring him back to me.

BLANCA. Who is he, *Ama*?

DOLORES. I'll tell you, honey, if you'll dance with me.

(BLANCA slow dances with DOLORES.)

Your father is a good dancer. He holds my hand like it's this little bird and makes me feel special. Every night he comes to my house and sometimes drives me to the barrios where I bring in the songs of little babies. On Sunday afternoons, he helps me collect herbs for my healing and plays with Pepín in the garden.

BLANCA. He plays with Pepín?

DOLORES. Oh he loves him so, and he loves the taste of fresh corn tortillas, and has a smile the wingspan of a sparrow, and he touches the place where you are being formed…

(**BLANCA** *places her hand on* **DOLORES**' *stomach.*)

BLANCA. Ohhh…

DOLORES. Shh, he says. No-one can know about us. We are a secret. Our love is a crime. Shh. Shh.

BLANCA. And then there is so much blood and lightning and then we are at the river

DOLORES. Deported in the worst of ways

BLANCA. On the worst of nights

DOLORES. Forced to swim across the *rio* like a wetback but backwards!

(**BLANCA** *roars back, ripping a knife out from the pocket of her coat.*)

BLANCA. WHERE ARE YOU, COBARDE! HOW CAN YOU LIVE WITH YOURSELF! I'LL RIP YOU TO PIECES!

DOLORES. If the blade fits, *mija.*

(*Voices off calling:* ALTO! ALTO! **BLANCA** *hides the knife and runs.* **DOLORES** *turns to see* **CELESTINO** *enter.*)

I dream a man dreaming of me and this creature with no arms no legs and no face, this creature called night is dreaming us.
"*Prefiero estar dormida que despierta…*"

(**DOLORES** *dances away. Lights up on Nextex.*)

CELESTINO. – "*De tanto que me duele que no estés.…*"

(**SONIA** *appears at her desk.*)

SONIA. I love how you sing to me, baby! *Dame un besito.*

(*He kisses her.*)

CELESTINO. How's my darling?

SONIA. Busy like hell. I got these *pinchi* mid-quarter reports to go through and its inventory time and then another girl in assembly went missing last night.

CELESTINO. Another one?

SONIA. Third one this month. Too bad, this Blanca Rosario was good. Tough to replace, that's for sure.

CELESTINO. So what's this about a call?

SONIA. It came early this morning about eight-thirty. I don't know how the call got routed.

CELESTINO. Who was it?

SONIA. You ever heard of Bustamante?

CELESTINO. No.

SONIA. That's the problem. Nobody has.

CELESTINO. So what did he want?

SONIA. She. It was a *pinchi* woman.

CELESTINO. The hell you say.

SONIA. She said she had a special shipment she wanted us to move for her. More *contrabanda* than you can dream in twenty years, she called it.

CELESTINO. What the hell does that mean?

SONIA. Nobody knows who this bitch is. Nobody has anything that big in the works.

CELESTINO. Then she's a crank.

SONIA. Not so fast, baby. This lady knows how we cut deals with the narcos, how we charge them a toll so that *pinchi* Frank and the INS look the other way at the *puente*.

CELESTINO. She knows this?

SONIA. And she knows they smuggle their shit in our trucks in TV boxes.

CELESTINO. *Cabrona.*

SONIA. She even offered to give us information on other local smuggling operations so Frank can bust their ass. Is this wild *o qué*?

CELESTINO. Keep checking her out. If she's for real, we'll know it soon enough.

SONIA. This woman freaks me out, *mi amor*.

CELESTINO. Let me worry about her. There's more pressing *negocio* afoot.

SONIA. Now what?

CELESTINO. Sonia, between you and me, I don't understand Mexico anymore. Juarez disagrees with me. And this factory, you deal with it more than I do nowadays. You make this maquila hum.

SONIA. Damn right.

CELESTINO. You got good people skills –

SONIA. Fire and hire!

CELESTINO. You're bilingual –

SONIA. English and html.

CELESTINO. And you know how I like things.

SONIA. Eggs hardboiled, cars imported, women four-alarm. What's your point?

CELESTINO. I need your help with a young man.

SONIA. What kind of help? Who's the young man?

CELESTINO. It's complicated. My…my son is home after a long absence and he's going to need some help adjusting.

SONIA. Hold the phone. I thought you said he was still-born.

CELESTINO. Only to the world. I'll explain it all later. Right now, I need your help.

SONIA. You mean, he needs a mother.

CELESTINO. There's a big change coming and I want you to be part of it. I looked at the charts and by the stars' conjunctions, you are there.

SONIA. What am I wearing?

CELESTINO. Silver, 16 million volts of flowing silver just above the knee, sandals, a brooch like a jaguar's eye, regal hair pinned back by regal hands.

SONIA. On my ring finger. Is the diamond one full carat?

CELESTINO. *(presenting her with a ring)* Two.

SONIA. Let's see the boy.

(The Robles Estate. FRANK *enters.)*

FRANK. That's not possible. I just had him washed and changed. He's sleeping it off.

CELESTINO. How is he?

FRANK. Sleeping it off. I guess you know the whole story.

SONIA. Oh yes. Maybe you should send the servants home till he gets better.

FRANK. Are you ordering me?

SONIA. Just a suggestion, Frank.

FRANK. I saw your bags in the hall. Does this mean you're moving in?

SONIA. Looks like it. Now you can spend more time with your family, I'm sure your wife misses you.

FRANK. Lady –

CELESTINO. Frank, Sonia is my wife now.

FRANK. Many happy returns.

SONIA. Gracias, Francis.

CELESTINO. We work as a team on our other enterprise. I expect us to work as a team here.

*(*FRANK*'s cell phone rings. He answers.)*

FRANK. Hello...Yeah? Who?...Hold on...You know a Bustamante?

SONIA. How did she get the number?

FRANK. Something about a shipment. Shit guaranteed to break your heart, her words.

CELESTINO. A poet.

FRANK. She's got some shit on a rival operation. Coming next week. She wants to rat these losers out as a sign of good faith.

CELESTINO. I don't talk with snitches. Take it, baby.

(**SONIA** *takes the phone and notates as* **SETH** *and* **CARL** *enter.*)

FRANK. Your hats, boys.

SETH. Mr. Robles.

CARL. Sir.

FRANK. What's the news, Carl?

CARL. Picked up a couple wets outside the city limits.

SETH. Young guys. Right off Highway 80.

FRANK. Any I.D. on them?

CARL. *Nada.* One of them's a retard but the other speaks English pretty good for a greaser.

CELESTINO. The term used in this house is Mexican.

CARL. Messican.

FRANK. Drive them to the station. We'll process them tonight.

CELESTINO. Wait. Bring them in, Frank. Let me see them.

FRANK. What for?

CELESTINO. I might need their services. Bring them in.

(**SETH** *and* **CARL** *go.*)

SONIA. *(clicking the phone off)* Done, *mi amor.* Time, place, tonnage, and caliber.

CELESTINO. Let's arrange a reception for these fuckers. No-one comes through my sector without my knowing. Or my fee.

FRANK. So you gonna tell me who this Bustamante is?

CELESTINO. In time, *compadre.*

(**SETH** *and* **CARL** *bring in* **ALFONSO** *and* **PEPÍN**.)

SETH. This is them.

FRANK. Which one of you's the retard? *(no response)* All right. Which one's the genius?

PEPÍN. Me, *señor.*

FRANK. How old are you?

PEPÍN. Many ages, *señor*. My feet are babies cause they came out last, my head's retired cause it came out first, my mouth's of drinking age, my hands old enough to drive, and my weenie is newborn every night.

FRANK. And you? You don't talk? That's a fine old hat. Where'd you get the hat, boy?

BLANCA. Hats R Us.

SETH. Musta stole it, this funny guy.

PEPÍN. *Oye*, I'm the funny! How many wetbacks does it take to screw in a lightbulb?

SETH. How many?

PEPÍN. I'm asking you, stupid.

(*PEPÍN roars with laughter.*)

SONIA. Where were you going?

BLANCA. Wherever they need pickers.

FRANK. What's this suitcase for, Jose?

BLANCA. It's Alfonso to you, *pendejo*!

PEPÍN. He don't have *chi-chis*.

CARL. (*striking him*) Shut up, retard!

BLANCA. *ORALE*, I TOLD YOU LEAVE HIM ALONE!

(*She jumps on CARL but FRANK grabs her.*)

FRANK. Boy, in case you ain't noticed, you're a *mojado* now, and in this state, *mojados* rate lower than dog. You understand?

BLANCA. I understand you're a *pinchi gringo* in a country fulla *pinchi gringos*, and I'd rather be dog than you any day!

(*FRANK takes out his gun, aims it at her. CELESTINO places his hand on FRANK's gun and slowly lowers it.*)

CELESTINO. Willful boy.

FRANK. Nobody's ever talked to me like that before.

BLANCA. How come we're here? How come you don't send us back?

CELESTINO. I have need of a tutor. Say yes, you get bed, board, and documents. Say no, you go back.

BLANCA. What a country. Who am I tutoring?

CELESTINO. My son. Lazaro. I'll have sandwiches in the kitchen for you.

FRANK. Put the Jerry Lewis in the car –

PEPÍN. NO! NO! ALFONSO! CARNAL!

BLANCA. Wait, he don't go nowhere without me! He's my brother!

CELESTINO. I only need one of you.

BLANCA. He won't take up room. He'll eat off my plate. He'll sleep with me.

PEPÍN. How many wetbacks does it take to change a bed?

CELESTINO. You start now.

(**CELESTINO** and **SONIA** go.)

CARL. Is he serious, Frank? Guy's one taco short of a combination plate.

FRANK. I'm sure you men will manage with him just fine.

SETH/CARL. WHUT! US? NO WAY!

PEPÍN. *¡Orale!*

(*Lights change.* **DOLORES** *over the sleeping* **LAZARO.**)

DOLORES. Embryos inside embryos inside embryos. Your dream is your chrysalis, a flicker of the eyelid your wing, your waking a pinch of this skin.

(*She pinches him and dances away.* **LAZARO** *stirs.*)

LAZARO. *Luz. Mas luz.* Too much *pinchi luz.*

(He takes in the newness. Feels his neck. Sees his arms.)

No chain. No pain.

(The fabric of his pajamas.)

Soft.

(He twists around and checks the label of his pajama top.)

Pierre Cardin. *Chingao*, this **is** heaven.

(CELESTINO steps forward.)

CELESTINO. Do you know me?

LAZARO. Are you God?

CELESTINO. I am your father.

LAZARO. ...father?

CELESTINO. You are my son. *Mi varon.* Born under *Centauro.* You don't remember me? You don't remember anything?

LAZARO. I remember being pissed about something.

(He feels CELESTINO's leather coat.)

Italian?

CELESTINO. Yes. Lazaro, *escuchame.* You've been very sick. You had a rare condition. For three weeks you've been sleeping.

LAZARO. Asleeping?

CELESTINO. Dreaming. You spoke of an island. And a chain. But there is no chain.

LAZARO. *¿Un sueño?*

CELESTINO. I missed you, boy. I missed you so much. A lifetime gone by.

LAZARO. No shit.

CELESTINO. I'll teach you. I'll make up for the lost time... *mijo.*

LAZARO. *Apa.*

(SONIA steps forward with her opened compact. She shows him his reflection.)

SONIA. Lazaro. *Mira.* This face, this young man....

(He is intrigued by the reflection. He sniffs the make-up.)

CELESTINO. This is Sonia, she's your –

SONIA. Mother. I'm your mother. Don't you know me?

LAZARO. I know Anne Klein.

(FRANK steps forward.)

Frank?

FRANK. Pilgrim.

LAZARO. You were in this dream. You were Tio Sugar who kept me chained. Shot me up with T-rex. Sent me on prickly death. You were a real fucker, Frank.

FRANK. Well, what can I tell you.

CELESTINO. Can you stand? Are you ready to see your house?

SONIA. It's real. Twenty-two rooms.

FRANK. Tino, I don't think it's a good idea. I don't think he's ready.

(LAZARO suddenly turns and lunges at FRANK.)

LAZARO. *PINCHI* FRANK! *TU ME CHINGASTE, CABRON! TU!*

(He latches onto FRANK's head and tears his ear off. CARL and SETH run in to separate them. LAZARO spits the ear out.)

SONIA. OH MY GOD!

CARL. JESUS H!

CELESTINO. LAZARO! Get him off! Stop it!

(They tear LAZARO off FRANK, who screams holding his bleeding head. LAZARO spits the gory mass on the floor.)

LAZARO. I WANT MY CHAIN! *MIS* COVER GIRLS! MY TV GUIDES! GO BACK! I WANNA GO BACK!

(He knocks **SETH** *and* **CARL** *to the floor and runs out.)*

SONIA. Oh my god! My god!

CELESTINO. He's an animal!

SONIA. What did you expect! He's been caged all his life!

FRANK. Goddammit! Can we talk about this later? Get me an ambulance!

CELESTINO. Get up and find him!

FRANK. He's going back, Tino! I'm putting him back!

SONIA. NO! He's just scared and confused!

LAZARO. *(off)* WHERE IS *MI ISLA!*

CELESTINO. *¡MADRE DE DIOS!*

*(***CELESTINO*** and ***SONIA*** rush out.)*

FRANK. Lord….I'm passin out….

*(***DOLORES*** enters with a jar bristling with herbs and wildflowers.)*

DOLORES. *Ruda, romero,* passion flower, yarrow. *Cascara sagrada, yerba buena.* yellow shame. All my remedies crowd the river banks, catching wind and drowsy bees on their buds. If you doze off, they'll catch your daydreams too.

FRANK. Dolores…

DOLORES. *(as she rubs some herb extract on his ear)* Rub a little self-heal on and the swelling will go down.

FRANK. I'm seein' things….

DOLORES. Me, too. I'm seeing that maybe if the sun stays warm, I might be coaxed on the grass and toward my girl's conception. It just seems like the thing to do.

FRANK. No….

DOLORES. Now, while Pepín's dipping his feet on the shore, digging up crayfish with his toes. I could hike my dress up and fuck or just keep picking *yerbas* all day.

FRANK. I never, never meant to...

(**DOLORES** *delicately picks up the ear.*)

DOLORES. Here's a rare and pretty one. I'll save you for my birth pains.

FRANK. Whut? Birth pains? What do you mean....?

(*She nimbly places it in her jar and seals it.*)

DOLORES. *Albacar*, bitterroot, y *linaza*. All these I'll save for the fevers of denial. Teas and *purgas* for the fevers of denial.

(*She smiles on* **FRANK**. *Lights change.* **BLANCA** *and* **PEPÍN** *eating sandwiches in the kitchen.*)

PEPÍN. Mm. Good. ¿*Y el tuyo?*

BLANCA. Good.

PEPÍN. I like baloney. Baloney is the best meat. You make baloney into many things. Baloney makes sun, baloney makes flower, baloney makes happy face....

BLANCA. Don't play with your food.

PEPÍN. What do you have?

BLANCA. Ham.

PEPÍN. You know, *carnal, hamon* is the best meat –

BLANCA. Pepín, that dream you had, the one before Ama died, you said you saw this man and a woman giving birth...

PEPÍN. ¡*Mamasangre!*

BLANCA. You don't remember their faces?

PEPÍN. It's all a big darkmess. Only one face I dismember.

BLANCA. Who?

PEPÍN. He was dark and quivery –

BLANCA. Yeah?

PEPÍN. Scary and glary –

BLANCA. Like Sincero?

PEPÍN. No, baloney. He was a big bloody piece of baloney...WWWAAAHHH!

BLANCA. You mean, the baby.

PEPÍN. WWAAHHH! He went, like a monster without any chones!

BLANCA. Don't eat my sandwich. I'm gonna see if there's a way outa here.

(**BLANCA** *goes.* **PEPÍN** *puts slices of baloney on his face and staggers around like a big monster.*)

PEPÍN. AWWOORR! GRRR! OOGA BOOOGA!

(**LAZARO** *enters. He takes the meat off* **PEPÍN**'s *face and eats it.*)

LAZARO. *Isla.* Where did *cabrones* put my island?

PEPÍN. I didn't take it.

LAZARO. *As if que si, as if que no,* they said a dream, but I don't believe it.

PEPÍN. *Oye, vato,* maybe you're a dream. My dream. Maybe I'm *mimis* and the baloney is making me see shit!

(**LAZARO** *eats* **BLANCA**'s *sandwich.*)

Hey! That's not yours!

LAZARO. Hungry.

PEPÍN. *Mano,* you gonna get me in trouble! Blanca's gonna be mad cause she'll think I ate her samwich cause you won't be here cause I'll wake up!

LAZARO. And maybe if I wake up, you won't be here!

PEPÍN. ¿*O si*? (*He leaps on* **LAZARO**.) Get back in my dream, duermevato!

LAZARO. ¡*Ya!* Get off me!

(They wrestle as **CARL** *and* **SETH** *enter.)*

CARL. Easy, *muchacho.*

SETH. Lookee here, Lazaro. TV Guide.

LAZARO. TV guide....

CARL. Survivor...

SETH. 20-20...

(He reaches for it. They knock him out.)

CARL. Smackdown!

(They carry him off.)

PEPÍN. *¡Chingao! Duermevato* fell outa my sleep and now he's the shit-kicky outa him! I gotta get him back in!

(He runs off. Lights change. **FRANK** *talks as* **CELESTINO** *scans his charts and peers through his telescope.)*

FRANK. I'm telling you, it was her! I saw her right before I passed out. She was gatherin' flowers and weeds.

CELESTINO. There. Disturbance in the field of Centaur.

FRANK. She said something about conceiving a girl. My daughter.

CELESTINO. A collision of star systems. He's on fire.

FRANK. Do you register what I'm saying? I saw her! She looked like she always did. Like I remember her.

CELESTINO. You remember her too fondly, Frank.

FRANK. Only woman I ever washed my truck for. Look, maybe his coming's got something to do with this.

CELESTINO. I have to make things right, Francis.

FRANK. For who? For you? Cause it ain't for him. He don't know how to act, he don't know thing one about being human!

CELESTINO. He'll learn.

FRANK. He'll learn that you let his mother die!

(**FRANK**'s *wound stings and thunder explodes. The lights change as* **DOLORES** *appears before him, her hands stained with blood.*)

DOLORES. *¿Que paso, baby?*

FRANK. Judas priest…

DOLORES. Why do you look at me like that?

FRANK. Dolores…

DOLORES. I did all I could, I swear.

CELESTINO. What's the matter with you? Vivian was your sister! That's her blood on her hands!

FRANK. I know, I know! JESUS!

CELESTINO. Pull your head out of your ass, fool! She's illegal! When are you going to tell your wife about her? When are you telling your blue-eyed babies? Does the agency know you're balling her every night?

FRANK. You wouldn't, Tino! You wouldn't!

DOLORES. *¿Que dicen?*

FRANK. Hold on, honey. *Un momento.*

CELESTINO. She can't ever come back and you can't go looking for her.

DOLORES. *¿Que pasa?*

FRANK. Dolores, Tino here is gonna drive you home. I have to stay with the baby and…

DOLORES. *Perdoname.* I did all I could.

FRANK. I know. I know. I'll meet you there.

DOLORES. Will you, *querido?*

FRANK. Count on it.

DOLORES. I waited for you, my love, all those years ago, even as the current took me and my sweet Pepín I waited for you to save us. I waited for you. I'm waiting for you still.

FRANK. I don't go there. I never go there. You know that.

DOLORES. *"Amor eterno, E inolvidable*
Tarde o temprano estaré contigo
Para segir, amándolos."

(She fades away and the lights resume.)

CELESTINO. Are you in love with a ghost, Frank?

FRANK. I hate you, as I hate him, as I hate all your god-damned race. And I reckon I'd despise her too if I didn't hate myself more.

(Lights change. **LAZARO** *hog-tied on his bed.* **BLANCA** *in a separate area.)*

LAZARO. No memory of my hole, my chain, my isla. But this room. This bed. These ropes. They remember me.

BLANCA. Trying to run. Stay with my cause. Sincero. Sangre. But I can't. Against my will, I go this way.

LAZARO. Something here was

BLANCA. Compelled by the suit

LAZARO. Dreamt in blood

BLANCA. Compelled by his shoes

LAZARO. A tearing of membrane

BLANCA. Legs obeying trousers

LAZARO. A mother's cry

BLANCA. Up the marble staircase

LAZARO. A womb on fire

BLANCA. Hallways like uterine canals

LAZARO. Bleeding on this bed

BLANCA. Through a bone-colored door

LAZARO. Parting of the legs

BLANCA. Opens like an eyelid opens

LAZARO. Opening

BLANCA. Slowly

LAZARO. Now

(They see each other: a recognition.)

BLANCA. Are you Lazaro?

LAZARO. Am I?

BLANCA. I'm Alfonso. I'm supposed to tutor you.

(They remain mesmerized by each other. So many recognitions.)

LAZARO. C'mere. In the light. *(She approaches.)* I seen you before?

BLANCA. I don't know you, *vato.* This is my first time in this house.

LAZARO. Bitchin.

BLANCA. How are you supposed to learn anything tied up like that?

LAZARO. I can learn about knots....

BLANCA. Get up.

(She begins to undo the ropes.)

LAZARO. You sure we never met?

BLANCA. Positive.

LAZARO. I was on this *isla* where I saw the strangest *locos.* Came and went like vapors.

BLANCA. Uh-huh.

LAZARO. Anyway, this one covergirl came up my shore.

BLANCA. A covergirl, huh?

LAZARO. *Bonita.* She rose from the water *y me dijo,* she said, you're gonna be free soon. She said to wait for her.

BLANCA. Maybe you should have.

LAZARO. She was something else. *Oye,* can I ask you, which do you read, *Elle* or *Esquire?*

BLANCA. Me?

LAZARO. *Elle* or *Esquire?*

BLANCA. *Motor Trend.* How's that?

LAZARO. Better.

BLANCA. What's that smell, man? Did you crap on yourself?

LAZARO. I had to go.

BLANCA. Man, you are too much. I don't know about this.

LAZARO. *Mira,* Alfonso.

BLANCA. Look, maybe I'm not cut out –

(She starts out. He knocks her down and sits on top of her.)

LAZARO. I'm all teeth today, *carnal,* clamp myself on that vein, make a red drape from your neck to the floor, *puto!*

BLANCA. Whatever, *vato!* Whatever!

LAZARO. Answer me one *cosa!*

BLANCA. Sure. Anything.

LAZARO. Am I *soniando?* Is this real?

BLANCA. It's real, brother.

LAZARO. Then okay. Teach me.

BLANCA. Get off.

*(**LAZARO** gets off her. **BLANCA** gets up, turns around and grabs **LAZARO** by the balls.)*

First lesson. When your body functions go, do not, I repeat, do not sit them on top of your tutor. It's a foul practice and it grosses me out. *¿Me oyes?*

LAZARO. I hear you.

BLANCA. Then okay. On to lesson two.

*(She drags him off. Crossfade to **SETH** and **CARL** with flashlights trained on the ground.)*

SETH. Now, tell me again, what's it look like?

CARL. Looks like a big ol' goddamned ear, Seth. Frank said it floated off so it floated off. Now hunt! Goddog!

(**PEPÍN** *enters.*)

PEPÍN. *Hey, migra!* Migra! Where is he? What did you do with him?

CARL. Fuck off, retard.

SETH. Hey, little guy.

PEPÍN. Where's my dreamvato, *ese? You* took him away!

SETH. What dreamvato?

CARL. Don't pay any attention to the retard, Seth! Git!

SETH. Hold on, Carl. Fella needs our assistance. I'm Seth and this is Carl.

PEPÍN. Thirst and Carol.

CARL. That's Carl. *Carl.*

SETH. You say he's the man of yer dreams?

PEPÍN. No, he fell out of my dreams. He was in my sueno but he got out!

SETH. Well, from the sound a things, I'd peg him for a illegal alien.

CARL. For crying Jesus!

SETH. He violated the borders of that territory, Carl! You just don't do that!

PEPÍN. That's right, *ese!* He's a dream *mojado!*

SETH. According to our mission statement, it's our duty to prevent unlawful entry, employment, or receipt of benefits by those who are not entitled to them.

PEPÍN. He ate my samwich!

SETH. And to apprehend and remove those aliens whose stay is not in the public interest.

PEPÍN. That sounds like him, Thirsty!

SETH. Brother, I suggest you enforce the departure of this individual as expeditiously as possible.

CARL. Retardo's a wet, too, in case you forgot.

SETH. Not if he's here to escape persecution. He can apply for asylum.

CARL. He looks like he already belongs in one.

PEPÍN. *¡Gracias, Carla!*

CARL. CARL!

SETH. I'll get a form I-589 from the car for you to fill out. In the meantime, buddy, raise your *mano.*

SETH. You pledge to uphold the Constitution of the United States of America and to obey its gun laws and such, and stand up for the National Anthem at ball games no matter who sings the damn thing? Say I do, *señor.*

PEPÍN. I do, *señor.*

SETH. You're now a citizen-patrol chief of the INS.

PEPÍN. *¡Hijola! ¡Un Americano!*

SETH. Now you're authorized to use whatever method it takes to nab your *mojado.* The method I recommend is D & D.

PEPÍN. D & D?

CARL. Detention and Deportation.

SETH. You gotta set your trap in order to **detain**, and once he's in custody, you **determine** his status and **deport** his ass back. Which kinda makes it D, D & D. Do you know the point of entry?

PEPÍN. The kitchen!

SETH. Then start the search there, chief. Cause that's where he's prob'ly stashed. You know what? I got something for you. Hold on.

(**SETH** *runs off.* **CARL** *searches for the ear.*)

PEPÍN. Carol, how come you so ugly?

CARL. What are you talking about? This is just my stern face. I wear this out on the field for protection. It's seen me through a few close calls.

PEPÍN. *¿De veras?*

CARL. Seth won't mention it cause he's jealous, but for outstanding service in the line of fire, I have received the Golden Huarache Award.

PEPÍN. Damn, *ese.* You mean, if I catch me a *mojado,* I can get a Golden Huarache too?

CARL. In your dreams.

PEPÍN. *Esuper!* Maybe if I get two *mojados,* I can get a pair of Huaraches!

(SETH returns.)

SETH. Okay, chief. Here's your form to fill out. Remember, you're persecuted. Try these out. Night vision scopes. With these babies on, there's no way in hell he'll dodge you.

(PEPÍN tries them on.)

PEPÍN. *¡Suavecito!*

CARL. Have you gone batty?

SETH. It's all in fun, Carl. C'mon. The State Department's gotta surplus of these. Besides, he may turn out to be a fine border scout.

PEPÍN. *(striking a pose with the night vision glasses on)* I am *La Migra!*

CARL. Little boys.

SETH. Wait till dark, chief, let the critter make his move. When you see him, pile-drive him headfirst back into your waking dreams. You got that?

PEPÍN. I am *La Migra!* Don't move, *joven,* I am *La pinchi Migra!*

SETH. Thass it! Meaner!

PEPÍN. I AM *LA MIGRA, CABRONES!*

(Lights change. BLANCA ushers LAZARO in, with a set of clothes. He dresses.)

BLANCA. I hear you been chewing on people's heads.

LAZARO. I was looking for something.

BLANCA. What kinda something?

LAZARO. Ideas. Ain't that where they come from?

BLANCA. Guys like you don't need ideas. You need a fucking leash.

LAZARO. 'nother chain.

BLANCA. A new chain, bro.

LAZARO. Still a chain.

BLANCA. Forged of new links, bro.

LAZARO. Chain's a chain.

BLANCA. Respect, charity, goodness, bro.

LAZARO. That ain't no chain, bro.

BLANCA. Love and faith and truth, bro.

LAZARO. Yeah right.

BLANCA. This is real shit, Laz, things that never change.

LAZARO. Only things that don't change are dead, bro.

BLANCA. Only if *la vida's* awol in your head, bro.

LAZARO. I don't wear truth around my neck, ese.

BLANCA. You wear it in your heart, or you're fucked. You wear it close to your soul or you die. Ground changes beneath you, people change their minds, but not truth. Keep it close, keep it tight, keep it shackled to your better sense.

LAZARO. My better self.

BLANCA. Fucking A. Chew my head, bite my ear off, rip my fuckin' heart to pieces. I'm all out of ideas.

LAZARO. But never never outa truth.

BLANCA. Right. On to Lesson three.

(**SONIA** *enters him with a small case.*)

SONIA. Is he washed?

BLANCA. Yes.

SONIA. Good. Do it often and fastidiously, your body is unclean to those who misunderstand you. You are your pigment. You'll be reminded of and judged by it for the rest of your *pinchi* life.

(She opens her case.)

My family was very poor living in the valley. There were eight of us *mocosos* in a little shanty, and being the youngest, I got all my sisters' old dresses. I was so second-hand in those rags, smelling of moth balls and rice. My hair thick in my face. And then one day I got a job selling –

(presents make-up supplies.)

….glamour.

LAZARO. Unbelievable!

SONIA. Check it out, baby. Eaus de toilettes – Parfums –

LAZARO. Face scrubs, scented soaps, bath oils – it's real…

SONIA. My articles of the Constitution. This is how you become American.

(She applies cream to his hands and face.)

I sold these over the counter at the mall. That's where I met your father. He offered me a job being manager at his maquiladora, his plant in Juarez. I almost said no.

LAZARO. Ay. The natural yet sultry feel that lasts and lasts.

(She applies hair gel.)

SONIA. Working with this gave me power, I could make new faces out of old, I could put Hollywood on the eyes of the brownest girl!

LAZARO. *Mi sueño.*

SONIA. *(daubing cologne on his face)* These are the talismans of beauty, Lazaro. These make the world bearable.

(She puts on his coat as the crowning touch to his new look.)

SONIA. *(cont.)* Remember, you're not a beast, a savage, a heathen, you are now fully Christian...Dior.

(**SONIA** *smiles, gives him a gentle kiss, and goes.*)

LAZARO. How do I look?

BLANCA. *Bien guapo.*

LAZARO. *¿Guapo?*

BLANCA. Time for Lesson Four.

(*Lights to black. A vision of the heavens appears.* **CELESTINO**'s *voice blares.*)

CELESTINO. *Lazaro Robles. Hijo Bravo.* This is your dominion...

(*He appears. A slide presentation commences.*)

Up there our fates are inscribed. Up there, the gods of antiquity slam down shots of *Patron* with the *dioses de mi* own mythology. Everything moves for the good of the Organism. There, the Great Bear, the Bull and the Dow Jones arrow between them, and over here Sun Microsystems. This is your *Mundo Comerciante.*

SONIA. Crown your head with knowledge. Everything a worldly man needs to know.

(**LAZARO** *is fed data via headphones and reading material.*)

FRANK/SETH/CARL. Texas History, Texas Monthly, Austin City Limits, Dallas Cowboys, price of oil per barrel, EDS, Bill Moyers, Wall Street Journal, Beemer 500 series.

SONIA. This is El Paso, gateway to the North, city on the cusp of Time.

FRANK. And this Juarez, back door to the Third World, to all parts Mexican.

CELESTINO. This is Rio Bravo, Rio Grande, Rio Polluted...

SONIA. The river that separates and binds the cities to el Organismo.

CELESTINO. And this is my grand enterprise, the NexMex Maquiladora. Our fine addition to the two-plant system of the US and Mexiconomies.

SONIA. One factory in El Paso for assembling parts by robotics. One factory in Juarez for assembling parts by hand. Together these plants collaborate to bring to America its finest contribution.

CELESTINO. Television.

FRANK. This is the US Border Patrol, an arm of the Immigration and Naturalization Service, sovereign protector of America's boundaries, watching out for illicit goods and persons. This agency stems the flood of narcotics threatening the Great Organism.

CELESTINO. But to keep pace with *traficantes*, we bargain with the Devil. A number of select cartels find safe passage north for a special toll and secret information on rival groups.

SONIA. This fee is funnelled into the NexMex account where it is recycled as clean money.

CELESTINO. As for those whom the heavens do not favor.

(**LAZARO** *is given night-vision specs. He puts them on, lights go black. The river at night. A handful of smugglers, masked and armed, dragging a small pontoon of packaged drugs. They stop when a large white light captures them and they raise their arms in surrender.*)

FRANK. *ALTO*, MOTHERFUCKERS!

CELESTINO. We tolerate some parasites and some we don't. Some lies valued as highly as truth, some truths dismissed as idle dreams, all for the sake of the Organism. These smugglers chose to keep the truth from me but I will not keep it from them. Say *fuego* and *fuego* comes.

LAZARO. Me?

CELESTINO. Say fire.

BLANCA. You can't cut them down like dogs. They're giving up!

LAZARO. I don't want to kill anyone, *Apa.*

CELESTINO. You're a Robles now. Say Fire!

BLANCA. You don't have to say anything.

LAZARO. WHAT DO I DO?

CELESTINO. Speak the truth! Say Fire!

BLANCA. Remember what I taught you!

LAZARO. This can't be real!

CELESTINO. THEN MAKE IT REAL!

> (**LAZARO** *struggles for a moment, then utters the cry.*)

LAZARO. *¡FUEGO!*

> (*Gunfire erupts. They are mowed down.* **SETH** *and* **CARL** *enter and drag the dead and their cargo off.* **LAZARO** *removes his specs.*)

Who is the Organism?

CELESTINO. You.

> (*Everyone goes, except* **LAZARO** *and* **BLANCA**. *She angrily drops his lunch at his feet.*)

BLANCA. Lunchtime.

> (*They sit.*)

LAZARO. I'm sorry. This world is hard to learn.

BLANCA. You're learning quick. Time for your American History.

> (*As he eats, she produces various items.*)

This is your father. This is you as a baby. The house you were born in. And you here at the ranch as a boy.

LAZARO. As a boy…

BLANCA. Here is your birth certificate. Your degree from SMU. Business Administration. Your membership into the El Paso Country Club.

LAZARO. Your hands are shaking.

(**BLANCA** *pulls them away and continues.*)

BLANCA. This is your passport. Driver's license, platinum card, and social security.

LAZARO. What does it mean?

BLANCA. It means you're set for life.

LAZARO. But is it my life? Do these things make me real?

BLANCA. The shit you make happen, that's what you are.

LAZARO. I didn't want to kill those men.

BLANCA. Then why?

LAZARO. It's what men do. They kill.

BLANCA. Didn't I teach you? Didn't I give you something to hold onto?

LAZARO. Words. Like from my radio on the isla.

BLANCA. Eat.

(*He eats.*)

You gotta learn to front off the bullshit, lie for lie, like I taught you. Ride your truth home. Cause home is all we got.

LAZARO. Where's your home?

BLANCA. Gone. I used to live in the *colonia* with a sick mother and brain-damaged boy. Leaving her passed out drunk in our one-room shanty so I could work in your dad's *maquila* while Pepín's doing dog tricks for the tourists. Going to the bathroom between cars. You don't want to know about my home.

LAZARO. It's more real than this.

BLANCA. Juarez? Give me a break.

LAZARO. What?

BLANCA. Over there, beyond the border freeway is a big town full of people with more reality than they can take. They live eat sleep within dreaming distance of this theme park called America. It draws them across the river like moths to the marquee. Then it burns them and chucks them back. So there's poverty violence and despair so thick in that city that even Mexico can barely claim it. Still the people thrive. Still they make the best of it. Playing and loving and dying in the shadow of this Dreamlandia.

*(***LAZARO*** gently kisses her.)*

Whoa, vato. What are you doing?

LAZARO. I can make you American. I can keep you here with me.

BLANCA. Shit…*mira,* first of all, men are not supposed to kiss, *sabes.*

LAZARO. Why not?

BLANCA. 'Cause…'cause…it's just the way it is. I can't get involved in this right now…

LAZARO. In that long dream that seemed to last my whole life, you were there as a woman. But here you are a man. Either way, you're the only real thing to me!

BLANCA. That's fucked! Listen up. You gotta get away from your *jefe.* Get away from all this. Its not real, its all a LIE. Even me, none of us are what we say we are.

LAZARO. A lie? You?

BLANCA. This crap ain't yours! I don't know whose it is, but it ain't yours! And that lady ain't your mother, neither! Lazaro, you gotta go. Leave all these fucking *mentiras* behind!

LAZARO. What are you talking about?

BLANCA. The island! It's real! Go out there, about three miles south along the bank and you'll see it! We've all made a fool of you.

LAZARO. Where are you going?

BLANCA. I have to get away from here! I can't breathe! I can't think straight! Oh my god!

LAZARO. Alfonso, wait!

BLANCA. Let go a my arm.

LAZARO. Don't leave me! You always leave me!

BLANCA. I can't stay!

LAZARO. I'm not letting you get away again! No way!

BLANCA. Lazaro.

LAZARO. NOT AGAIN, DREAMFUCK!

(He knocks her roughly on the ground and tries to kiss her.)

BLANCA. STOP IT LAZARO! DON'T TOUCH ME!

LAZARO. I WANT YOU! *¡SOMOS IGUALES!*

BLANCA. GET OFF!

*(**BLANCA** scrambles to her feet and pulls out her knife. **SETH** and **CARL** rush in and grab her. **CELESTINO** enters behind them. He goes directly to **LAZARO** and violently grabs him.)*

CELESTINO. New lesson. Beware the illegal. The most disposable. The most *invisible.* They slip in through our lawns, our kitchens, our *hoteles y restaurantes.* They lack identity so they abuse ours. America can't afford to be soft on them.

BLANCA. Fuck you! You're more of a wetback than we are!

CELESTINO. I'm not a wet.

*(**BLANCA** spits on him.)*

BLANCA. You are now.

CELESTINO. Save this little *puto* for me.

(**SETH** *and* **CARL** *take* **BLANCA** *away.*)

BLANCA. *(as she is dragged off)* It's real, Lazaro! Go there! See for yourself! See for yourself!

CELESTINO. *(to* **LAZARO***)* Don't make me believe in curses again.

(*He goes.* **LAZARO** *remains. Lights shift to the island.* **DOLORES** *quietly waits by his hovel.*)

LAZARO. Real. My *isla.*

(*He drags his chain out and feels its links.* **DOLO-RES** *strews the herbs and flowers of her jar in a wide arc around him.*)

No dream.

DOLORES. *Aqui. La hora de tu ser.*

LAZARO. What have I been living? *¿Y porque?*

DOLORES. *Eres cruzado, cruzando el rio, el cielo, la tierra, y el Corazon.*

LAZARO. Less than a dog's life, a lie, a filthy lie repeated day after day after *dia y dia y dia....*

(**LAZARO** *falls weeping.* **DOLORES** *stands over him.*)

DOLORES. Now the son comes for his second birth!

(*She takes his head and pulls. He cries out.*)

LAZARO. No! I don't want it! I don't want to see!

DOLORES. We shed light as we shed blood.

LAZARO. I don't want this life!

DOLORES. *¡Ahora, maldicion, vas a dar luz!*

LAZARO. NO! NOO!

DOLORES. I dug my nails in you once!

(**LAZARO** *cries out.*)

I dug my nails in your skull! You wear the marks like a crown of thorns!

LAZARO. NOOO!

DOLORES. Now I bring you in to be my fire!

(She stands him to his full abominable height.)

LAZARO. *¡CABRONES! ¡PINCHIS MENDIGOS! ¡Si asi es, asi es!* So be fuckin it! You want me to live these lies, fine! I will manifest you by the book! Up the ass! You gonna see this Cover Boy shine! You gonna see this Cover Boy flame! You gonna see this Cover Boy BURN!

(blackout)

End Act One

ACT TWO

(Darkness. The riverbank. PEPÍN wearing the night-vision goggles.)

PEPÍN. I am *La Migra.*

I detain, determine, deport. Keep the *mojados al otro lado.* Don't put your brown on my ground, *vato!*

(Stillness. He grows apprehensive.)

¡Trucha! Who's slimppin shadows by me? *¿Eres tu, sueño* man? You think it over, *hombre,* I got my goggles on for *Yankeelandia!*

(murmurs all around him)

Who's there! *¡Alto! ¡Manos arriba! ¡Le doy un* kick *en el* weenie!

(Shadowy figures emerge from the darkness.)

Detain, determine, deport. Detain, determine, de…

(PEPÍN sees images of border-crossers creeping past him.)

¡MIRA! Fantasmas, ghost crossers wading through the *rio.* Girls riding on the backs of men, old *rancheros* with their *botas* held high, young *chavalos* linking hands from one hell to the other, mothers with bundles held to their bosoms. Guided by the *lancheros* and the little stars reflected on the water, the desperate, the hungry, the hopeless, the dreams of the dead crossing.

(DOLORES emerges from the group of ghost-crossers.)

Mama. What you doing with these spookies?

DOLORES. Looking for her, *mijo*. Belladonna hides in clumps along the shores.

PEPÍN. Belladonna?

DOLORES. Pretty lady with the kiss of death.

PEPÍN. Never kissed me, Ma.

DOLORES. But you kissed her, Pepín. Cupful of death, half a cup of madness. *Ah, mira. Here it is.*

PEPÍN. Leaves like angel wings.

DOLORES. I ground them to make a tea for myself. It was never meant for you. A cupful of death.

PEPÍN. Half a cuppa madness.

DOLORES. *(rubbing the leaf against his heart)* I'll brew more of this. Someone's heart will need the bracing of this herb.

PEPÍN. OOFAS! Lookit where you're standing, *Jefita*! Right on the *linea* between U.S. And U Lose. As a citizen escout of the Border Patrol, I demand your *papeles, Mami!*

DOLORES. Here.

(She places the ear in his hand and goes.)

PEPÍN. Eerie.

(noise from off)

Oofahs! *Otros* spooky *vatos!*

*(He hides as **SETH** and **CARL** drag **BLANCA** on. **FRANK** behind.)*

BLANCA. Get your paws offa me! Does Robles own alla you dogs or do you think for yourselves sometimes?

CARL. Aw don't be so glum, Al, this is better for all a us.

SETH. Nothing personal, y'understand.

CARL. Mr. Robles just don't appreciate your teaching style.

SETH. So he hereby relieves you of your duties.

BLANCA. What you gonna do? Gun me down, leave me for the turkey hawks? Why don't you say something?

FRANK. *(produces the knife)* Where did you get this?

BLANCA. It's mine.

FRANK. WHERE DID YOU GET IT?

BLANCA. GO TO HELL, GRINGO!

FRANK. Mr. Robles asked that you be found right here in possession of this blade, this controlled substance and a couple Smith and Wesson slugs. Now, I might decide to skip the slugs if you come clean about the damn knife.

BLANCA. It belongs to Sincero.

FRANK. Sincero.

BLANCA. You know him?

FRANK. What's he to you? How do you know him? Spill the refrieds.

BLANCA. All these questions. He's suppose to be my *jefe.*

FRANK. Your father…

BLANCA. *Puro cabrón.* I got no stomach to see him, but I need to.

FRANK. Boy, you already have. This is my knife.

BLANCA. Wait a minute. You?

FRANK. Given to me when I joined the *Migra.*

BLANCA. You can't be Sincero.

FRANK. You can't be my son. But there you are saying it.

BLANCA. You're a gringo.

FRANK. You're a by-god wetback. How do I know you're not dicking with me? Playing up to my weakness.

BLANCA. My mother's name is Dolores.

FRANK. And she was my weakness.

BLANCA. How can you be him? I don't get it.

FRANK. Frank in Spanish is Sincero, you damn fool! Frank, sincere. Sincero. Your mama's idea of irony! Where is she?

BLANCA. Dead.

FRANK. Then Tino was right. Are you mine, then?

BLANCA. Oh shit, kill me! Shoot me! I don't wanna hear this!

FRANK. Is that idiot boy my Pepín?

BLANCA. Shoot me! God! Don't tell me any more!

SETH. Chief, what you gonna do? You got orders to cap yer own bloodkin.

CARL. And yer son's got cause to geld you, too.

FRANK. *(revealing her hair)* Except he ain't my son. You're my daughter.

SETH. Whut! No effin' way!

FRANK. You're my girl, ain't you?

BLANCA. *¡Gringa!* Everything I ever hated! *¡Soy pinchi gringa tambien!*

(She runs into the river.)

FRANK. WAIT! I WON'T HURT YOU! I JUST WANNA TALK!

BLANCA. Wash away, wash away!

FRANK. IT'S DARK OUT THERE. YOU'LL DROWN.

BLANCA. Drown this body, erase me! Suck the whiteness off!

FRANK. Get in there and find her.

CARL. I ain't goin' in there!

(The waters sweep her away. PEPÍN leaps out in alarm.)

PEPÍN. *¡BLANCA!*

FRANK. *(catching him)* Whoa, sonny! Did you call her Blanca? Is that her name? Answer me!

PEPÍN. Blanca…

(He catches him. Recognizes him.)

FRANK. I'll be damned. Is that her name? Blanca? Haul him back to the compound. And keep yer yaps shut about this till I talk with him!

*(**SETH** and **CARL** take him off. **FRANK** slashes the dark with the flashlight beam.)*

COME BACK! I WANNA TALK! FER CRYING JESUS, DOLORES, WHATTA YOU DONE TO ME!

*(Lights change. **CELESTINO** and **SONIA** enter.)*

CELESTINO. I can't believe it. My own son.

SONIA. Tino, I don't think you have the whole picture –

CELESTINO. I give him everything he needs to be my exemplary boy. education, money, stock options, and what does he turn out to be? *Maricón.*

SONIA. What do you expect? What experience has he ever had with women? Fashion magazines!

CELESTINO. My son is not a *maricón*!

SONIA. Baby, trust me. I know what he likes, and it's not other men.

(Her cell phone rings. She answers.)

Diga. Her again.

(She passes the phone.)

CELESTINO. Bustamante, you're a ball-buster. *(pause)* Yes, your information was accurate. We took care of them. But that won't make us bedfellows. *(pause)* And if I say no? *(pause)* Let's assume then I say yes. Where do we meet and when? There? You want to meet there?

*(Pause. He shuts off the phone and hands it to **SONIA**.)*

SONIA. Well?

CELESTINO. The terms are decent.

SONIA. What did she hold over you, mi amor?

CELESTINO. The usual bullshit.

(**LAZARO** *bursts in.*)

LAZARO. *Papá.* What have you done with Alfonso? Where is he?

CELESTINO. *¿Buenos dias, mijo, como estas?*

LAZARO. Where have you taken him?

SONIA. Good morning, Lazaro.

LAZARO. *Mama,* where is he? All his things are gone.

CELESTINO. He had to go, *hijo.* His Visa ran out.

LAZARO. You deported him, didn't you?

SONIA. He wanted to go home –

LAZARO. Lies! He said they were all lies!

CELESTINO. *¡Está bien!* The truth is he's dead. The truth is he was a *maricón,* and no-one turns my son into a *maricón.* I never would have brought you back from that –

SONIA. Tino…

CELESTINO. (*gripping him by the throat*) …I raised you to be a man! Be a man!

LAZARO. I like that. I like your hand on my throat. It feels like a chain. I wake up in the middle of the night missing the cold steel on my skin. But then I remember I have you. My great dad. I like your hand on my throat.

(**SETH** *and* **CARL** *enter dragging* **PEPÍN** *in.*)

CARL. Shake a leg, retard!

SETH. Quit yer wiggling, chief!

PEPÍN. NO! You swored me in, you made me citizen chief, *la Migra!*

(**PEPÍN** *collapses in a heap before them.*)

CELESTINO. *¡Chingao!* Didn't I say I wanted them both taken care of?

CARL. I know, sir, but Frank said to bring him.

SONIA. What for?

SETH. Just said bring and we brung.

PEPÍN. Please, Thirst, let me keep the googles! I haven't found my *duermevato* yet!

SETH. Sorry, chief.

PEPÍN. *¡Mira! ¡Duermevato!* Here at last! Now I'll get my Golden *Huarache!*

(**PEPÍN** *goes for* **LAZARO**. *He gives him a vicious blow.*)

LAZARO. This is an illegal. A burden on this land. The most disposable. The most invisible.

(**LAZARO** *grabs* **PEPÍN**'*s leg and slowly twists it around.*)

These people are a world removed, *verdad, Papa?* Isn't that what you said?

(**PEPÍN**'*s leg snaps and he passes out.* **FRANK** *enters.*)

SETH. Jesus wept.

SONIA. That's enough, Lazaro.

FRANK. What's going on? What the hell have you done to him?

CELESTINO. I underestimated you.

SONIA. Get him out of here.

(**SETH** *and* **CARL** *carry* **PEPÍN** *off.* **FRANK** *glares at* **LAZARO**.)

FRANK. You shit.

CELESTINO. Get over it, Frank. I need you and Sonia in Juarez.

FRANK. Me?

CELESTINO. J-town, Francis. We have a date with Doña
Bustamante.

FRANK. Are you outa yer head? You know damn well I
don't go there.

CELESTINO. Better change the uniform.

FRANK. I don't go. You know I don't go. I never go.

CELESTINO. Sonia will accompany you.

FRANK. I don't trust her.

SONIA. Ha!

LAZARO. Let me go.

FRANK. You?

LAZARO. I want to see the other side. Mexico and the
maquila.

FRANK. Are you kidding me?

SONIA. What can it hurt?

CELESTINO. *Mijo,* everything in my life has been for
you. Will you be my centaur?

LAZARO. Whatever you want me to be, *Padre.*

SONIA. *It's settled.* Juarilandia!

*(Lights change. **BLANCA** enters, putting on a white
smock, white rubber shoes and gloves, hairnet, and
surgical mask.)*

BLANCA. Races, *Ama,* these races, they grow fathers,
mothers, daughters, sons and gods, these *raices*
brown as book, white as bone, black as tar, they
tell us who we are and punish what we're not. I'm
brown, I'm *India,* then Spanish, then white, or half
white which is worse than being all, I am all, Ama,
all that I denied is me! What am I? What race
dries up and another grows? I saw him, saw the
blood with blood matched up and it was mine. I'm
a white lie, lie of this Sincero, his half-truth, half-
breed, half Blanca, all *desmadre*! My father with his
raza stripped mine off and slipped me half of his
and left me with no race at all.

In this *maquila*, rebuild yourself. Out of parts imported from the north, make yourself new. This time without the *raza*.

(She puts on her surgical mask. Lights shift. **LAZARO**, **FRANK** *and* **SONIA** *enter.)*

LAZARO. The Threshold

FRANK. Border checkpoint

SONIA. To another world

LAZARO. Strange world

FRANK. Illegitimate culture

SONIA. *Ciudad Juarez, Chihuahua*

LAZARO. A city shaped like music

SONIA. Ground out of daily life

FRANK. Terrible, perilous music

LAZARO. Earthy, rich, spilling from cars and open doorways

FRANK. The smell of old meat, gasoline, piss

LAZARO. The smell of perseverance, of people, of business

SONIA. And the garish walls

LAZARO. Painted like parrots and iguanas in Benetton colors

FRANK. Random and flaking

LAZARO. Orgies of cars on the roads

SONIA. *Chavalitos* hawking *Chiclet*, cigarettes, rings of *plata*

LAZARO. Their dusty faces artifacts of me, burnt the brown of *centavos*

FRANK. Faces I have all expelled before

SONIA. And fruit stands and kiosks and vendors of ice

LAZARO. Churches with crumbling saints, Martin, Jose, Luis, Francisco

FRANK. Faces, swarms of faces, all of them sons and migrants

LAZARO. A messiness of living, a riot of language, old world in a new dream.

SONIA. I don't like it. Can we go to the hotel?

(Lights change. The silence of their hotel room. **FRANK** *is anxious.)*

You have to watch your purse or they'll rob you blind. Don't drink the water, don't get in taxis, don't stay out past dark, and always haggle. Haggling and *la mordida*, the bribe, are the two laws of this country.

FRANK. So where is she?

SONIA. We just got here. She'll call. Relax.

FRANK. If I'm not in my room, I'm at the bar.

*(***FRANK*** goes.)*

SONIA. It's hot. Open a window.

LAZARO. It's open.

SONIA. You want to take this room or the one next door?

LAZARO. Either one.

SONIA. When she calls, stay in your room. Don't come unless I say so.

LAZARO. *(his coat)* Feel this. Italian.

SONIA. You think you're pretty hot after that performance with Pepin, but these people are no idiots. If she's half like the fucks we deal with, she's watching us right now. You hear me?

LAZARO. In the town, *en el aire*, in the people, this ripeness. Everyone in heat. Even here, this table, two flies pinned together, oblivious to danger, passion too small to see. So dangerous, so blind to reality, two flies making fly-love.

SONIA. *Asi es la vida, Lazaro.*

(He slams his hand, smears it across the table top.)

LAZARO. You think she saw this?

SONIA. *¿Que te pasa, mijo?*

LAZARO. I don't like you calling me *mijo*.

SONIA. *Pero sabes muy bien que tu eres –*

LAZARO. *Lazaro. Y tu eres Sonia.*

SONIA. I'll take the other room.

LAZARO. How old are you? Almost half as old as my father?

SONIA. Older than you.

LAZARO. Not by much. I see how you look at me. Not with a mother's attention but attention to other *cositas*.

SONIA. You flatter yourself.

LAZARO. Rub more of that cream on me. Run those hands down my back again.

SONIA. You're not playing fair.

LAZARO. I'm not playing.

SONIA. You're not the son I thought you were.

LAZARO. Lovers never are.

SONIA. I have a lover already.

LAZARO. Buy get one free.

SONIA. Sounds like a bargain –

LAZARO. You said I should haggle.

SONIA. For a haggler, you don't give an inch.

LAZARO. An inch is all I need.

(They kiss and he mounts her on the bed. **CELES-TINO** *and* **FRANK** *enter on either side of them with phones.)*

FRANK. There's no word from Bustamante.

CELESTINO. Be patient.

FRANK. What the hell are we doing here? Why are we dealing with some damn woman we never met?

CELESTINO. Think of it as a test, Frank.

FRANK. I see in the faces of all this teeming Mexico my verdict. The undocumented of all my life. Now their eyes document me, make me the alien.

CELESTINO. Tell Sonia to give you and Lazaro a tour of the plant. He should know it.

FRANK. They sure spend a lotta time together.

LAZARO. *(making love to her)* ¡ASI!

CELESTINO. Mindful of the time, Frank. Mindful. The skies are a whorehouse tonight, all constellations in thermonuclear heat, the Archer's arrow in Andromeda's mouth, Aries ramming the back end of Orion while his dogs do each other, and even my Centaur mounts the Lady, Frank, roaring into Virgo's crease, pounding away, disgusting. *las estrellas Francisco*, are brimming with betrayal!

(Lights shift. The Maquiladora. **BLANCA** *at a table. Connecting colored wires to corresponding sockets. A voice on the speaker barks incomprehensible commands.)*

BLANCA. My new world order.

*(***SONIA** *leads* **LAZARO** *and* **FRANK** *through.)*

SONIA. My office is this way. Don't mind the workers.

*(***LAZARO** *approaches the platform where* **BLANCA** *works.)*

LAZARO. What are you doing?

BLANCA. *No hablo Ingles, señor.*

SONIA. *Mas respeto.* This is Sr. Robles.

*(***BLANCA** *nods deferentially.)*

FRANK. Can we move on? It's warm in here.

LAZARO. What's she's working on?

SONIA. Television circuit boards.

LAZARO. How much is she paid?

SONIA. Well enough.

BLANCA. Five dollars.

FRANK. You do speak English.

LAZARO. Five dollars an hour?

BLANCA. A day.

LAZARO. Take off that thing.

BLANCA. I can't, *señor*. Regulations.

LAZARO. How do you like your work?

BLANCA. *Oh, señor,* putting wires into sockets ten hours a day, very exciting.

LAZARO. Maybe you should get a raise.

BLANCA. Oh no. A raise is what unions want, but when *la policia* shoots its leaders and makes everyone sign retractions, it becomes clear. We don't need a raise. Everything is *suave.*

LAZARO. Is my father aware of this?

SONIA. He mobilized the police.

BLANCA. I like making TVs, *Señor Robles*, make no mistake. Dreams shine in these boxes, American dreams *para gente importante* like you. I make it possible to bring into your house *el* Bugs Bunny.

LAZARO. You have one?

BLANCA. No, *señor.* But the extra cardboard boxes they come in make fine insulation for my house.

FRANK. Have I seen you before?

BLANCA. Not likely. I've lived in *La Colonia Insurgentes* all my life.

SONIA. One of the cardboard settlements of *la cuidad.*

FRANK. You do look familiar....

BLANCA. We all look the same, *patron. Con su permiso.*

(She goes back to work.)

SONIA. We employ about two thousand women, but there's a large turnover. A lot of these girls go missing.

LAZARO. How?

SONIA. Rape. Murder. They work late hours, walk long miles across barren desert *lotes.* Many for the last time.

LAZARO. Serial killer?

SONIA. Serial machismo.

(They go. **FRANK** *returns to* **BLANCA,** *slowly removing her mask.)*

FRANK. I been seeing things all day. So I know it can't be you. But maybe pity lives in the delusions of a crazed old man. I don't shun what I got coming. I compromised my badge, my heart, and my sister's life for Lazaro. Your cousin. I'm a craven fuck. I know that. But I never meant your mama harm. I loved her. A dose of mercy might could ease my load. But if you're not so inclined, you might do what I'm too coward to administer myself.

(He gives her the knife. A moment. She puts the knife down.)

Sorry, miss. I mistook you. You look like someone I never knew.

(He goes out a different way. She grabs the knife.)

BLANCA. *Ama,* where is it! Where is the coraje, the need to hurt! Where is it! Why should I pity this man? His confession? His repentance? What makes white men repent their whiteness! God, that touch, that look in his eye, they erase everything, they form this need in me for father. For the first time...*padre...*

(She runs. Lights shift to the Estate. **SETH** *and* **CARL** *with* **PEPÍN.** *He lies with his head buried in his arms.)*

SETH. Talk to him, Carl.

CARL. You talk to him.

SETH. How's your leg, chief? Lissen, little buddy. I know what we said, but you gotta unnerstand, we were only funnin'.

CARL. We got no power to make you one of us. Only power we got is to make you one of them.

SETH. You're gonna have to go back now.

CARL. Back to Mexico.

SETH. We'll give you a ride, though. In our SUV. Whattaya say?

PEPÍN. Can I keep the googles?

CARL. No way. No way, Seth.

SETH. It's for his own pertection, Carl. Nighttimes out there in Mexico are fulla evil hazards, mark my words!

CARL. Hazards like whut?

SETH. The *chupacabra*.

CARL. *Chupa-whut?*

SETH. A wicked creature born of industrial pollution and the evil spell of *Santería*.

CARL. You kiddin', right?

SETH. The thing about this *chupacabra* is it sucks the blood of goats without spilling a drop. Once, I swear to God, one time it jumped a Texas Ranger while he was on patrol. Drained the body of blood. Looked like the husk of a two-week old *tamale*.

(**CELESTINO** *enters.*)

CELESTINO. Leave us.

(**SETH** *and* **CARL** *go.*)

I know you. It took a while but I remember. You're the *bruja*'s son. You were there the night she delivered Lazaro. How is your *mama*? You wanna call her on the phone?

(*He takes out his celphone. Pretends to dial.*)

CELESTINO. Pi-pa-pi-pa-pa-pa-pi-pi-pa-pa-pi.

Bueno. Sra. Dolores Midwife? I have your little *payasito* right here. You wanna have a word?

(He gives the phone to **PEPÍN**. *He speaks in falsetto.)*

Alló, Pepín. How your leg? Brusha your teeth. Say your *Padre Nuestros* and make the man happy. *Adios mijo. Cleeck.*

(He puts the phone down.)

Mama dead.

PEPÍN. *Muerta?*

CELESTINO. It's up to me to care for you. But you have to help me. Who's that young man Alfonso? Why did he come?

PEPÍN. *No puedo.*

CELESTINO. What? *No pedo? No pedo?*

*(**CELESTINO** lifts his leg and makes a farting noise.)*

Prrt. *Si Pedo.*

PEPÍN. *Huh?*

CELESTINO. BPLLFFT!

*(**PEPÍN** snickers.)*

PPPPPPPPRRRRFFTTT!

(The fart propels him to his feet.)

¡Pedo Americano! You try.

PEPÍN. *(raising a hip)* psssst.....

CELESTINO. *¡PEDORRO!*

PEPÍN/CELESTINO. PRRTTTT! PRRRRT! PRRRT! PRRRRRT!

*(They parade around arm in arm until **PEPÍN** falls in pain.)*

PEPÍN. AAAY-AYY-AYY-AYYY!

CELESTINO. Sorry, sorry, sorry. Can I tell you a secret? When I was a *chavo*, I was like you. I used to dress up like a clown and do silly tricks for *centavos*. Juggle. Magic. Breathe fire with real gasoline. It ruined my lungs.

PEPÍN. You?

CELESTINO. Humiliation is standing between lanes of cars aimed toward the US, while all the clean Anglo faces pass by me and my stupid tricks.

PEPÍN. *Chiste.*

CELESTINO. I might have killed myself on solvents and glue, except an old white couple swept me into their car and smuggled me past Immigration. That's my secret, Pepín. I no American.

PEPÍN. *You a Mexicano?*

CELESTINO. That's what Bustamante called me over the phone. "Mexicano, you murdered your own wife. To hide your roots, she died." Specious accusation. But how did she know?

PEPÍN. *¿Eres mojado?* Like me?

CELESTINO. *Pedo* is a fine Spanish word, meaning gas to some, drunkenness to others, bullshit to yet other people. But the translation for *pedo* I prefer is **trouble**. *(stepping on his broken leg) VA VER **PEDO** SI NO ME DICES DE **ALFONSO**.* I see how Frank looks at you! He brought you back for a reason. Something lives between all you fuckers. Now talk!

PEPÍN. Don't hurt me! Please! *¡No Pedo!* Alfonso the mister....

CELESTINO. Yes?

PEPÍN. Is really my sister.

(*Lights change. The Board room.* SONIA *and* LAZARO.)

SONIA. So where the hell is she? And where did Frank wander off to?

LAZARO. We don't need him.

SONIA. Fuck. Everyone's running on Chicano time.

LAZARO. How long have you and my father been together?

SONIA. A few years.

LAZARO. Did you know he had me put away? I've seen the island, the chain.

SONIA. I didn't know anything. I didn't know your father could be like that, and to his own kid. It's like I never knew him.

LAZARO. You played along with the lies.

SONIA. So have you. We all play along or else how could we live? We make ourselves believe its not so till it's not.

(**BUSTAMANTE** *enters.*)

BUSTAMANTE. *Buenas noches.*

LAZARO. Doña Bustamante.

BUSTAMANTE. In the flesh, *cabrones.*

SONIA. About time.

BUSTAMANTE. Okay. You're the midlevel bitch, so you must be the *Patron. Sr.* Robles the badass magnate. Kinda young to be fucking around with the *toros, no?*

LAZARO. *Lazaro Robles.* I come on my father's behalf.

SONIA. No, he doesn't. You deal with me.

BUSTAMANTE. But I like the smell of young Robles.

SONIA. We keep him out of this or we don't deal at all.

BUSTAMANTE. *(pulling a gun)* Then deal with this, *babosa.*

SONIA. That won't solve a damn thing and you know it.

BUSTAMANTE. Maybe not over there, *pocha,* but over here, it solves everything.

LAZARO. You've made your point. Put it away.

BUSTAMANTE. But I haven't made my point.

LAZARO. Then maybe you should. We're on a schedule.

BUSTAMANTE. *Tambien yo, Robles. Tambien yo.*

*(She tosses the gun to **LAZARO**. Takes out her cell phone.)*

This is my third ear. It connects me to all of Mexico. Direct to a satellite called *Solidaridad.* Solidarity. An electronic Quetzalquatl soaring over its people. Big saucer-shaped eyes transmitting images and cries of *los Mexicanos.* Calls to action, to prayer, to the harvest of this fucking crop called *coca,* they all come here via Solidarity. Can you take my world, Robles, or are you pussy-gringofied?

LAZARO. Dale gas.

*(**BUSTAMANTE** dials her phone. **LAZARO***'s cell phone rings. He answers.)*

LAZARO. Noise.

BUSTAMANTE. That's right.

LAZARO. Corruption.

BUSTAMANTE. Go on.

LAZARO. Pops and wheezes.

BUSTAMANTE. Sounds of hunger.

LAZARO. Despair.

BUSTAMANTE. Slaughter.

LAZARO. Call-waiting.

BUSTAMANTE. Wait no more. Listen. Listen.

LAZARO. I hear…insurgence.

BUSTAMANTE. Yes.

LAZARO. Coming on a wide bandwidth.

BUSTAMANTE. Digital aliens.

LAZARO. A million people of indeterminate flesh.

BUSTAMANTE. Roaring into your ear.

LAZARO. My brain, my heart.

BUSTAMANTE. Busting through your walls, fences, surveillance towers.

LAZARO. Overrunning me.

BUSTAMANTE. Sucking up your light, your strength, your water.

LAZARO. Taking over me.

BUSTAMANTE. The totems of the new culture. the corrupt leaders, presidents, generals, police, college deans, narco bosses –

LAZARO. Los CEO's de multinational corpse and Citibank executives on Telemundo, a silicon breast in each hand –

BUSTAMANTE. *¡Asi mero!*

LAZARO. All of them calling the shots.

BUSTAMANTE. And what else!

LAZARO. Real life day of the dead *calacas* begging for dog food

BUSTAMANTE. *¿Y que mas?*

LAZARO. Poor children trading ATM cards for coca

BUSTAMANTE. *¡Y que Mas!*

LAZARO. Cops moonlighting as narco bodyguards!

BUSTAMANTE. *¡Y QUE MAS!*

LAZARO. *La Virgen de Guadalupe* whoring herself for a fix!

BUSTAMANTE. Now you got it!

LAZARO. Money, narcotics, crime, industrial waste, human cargo!

BUSTAMANTE. HA HA!

LAZARO. All of them laughing, laughing at the drug war, the legislation, the just-say-nos, the Founding Fathers of the DEA –

BUSTAMANTE. HAHAHA!

LAZARO. Laughing like skulls at the Privilege which spawned it all and now pray for it to stop, as if the bleeding ever stops, as if the music ever stops –

BUSTAMANTE. It's a dance, *machoman*, with a techno-beat between two countries posing in the mirror

LAZARO. Only which is the real

BUSTAMANTE; Which the *sueño*

LAZARO. As if *que si*

BUSTAMANTE. As if *que no*

LAZARO. Are you mah bitch?

BUSTAMANTE. No, you mah bitch now!

LAZARO. Yes!

BUSTAMANTE. We the best export, the true ambassadors.

LAZARO. The real Zapatistas of these twisted times.

BUSTAMANTE. 'Cause the real narcotic is **hope**, smuggled in body cavities they will NEVER reach, muthafukkah.

LAZARO. And one awesome apoca-lipstick day

BUSTAMANTE. All the cell phones, yours and mine

LAZARO. Gonna wail on the very same line.

BUSTAMANTE. Solidarity.

(**LAZARO** *clicks the cell phones off. Silence.*)

SONIA. *(dryly)* Ay….. Que sexy.

BUSTAMANTE. Now are you made.

LAZARO. What is it you want?

BUSTAMANTE. Give me Celestino. I give you the keys to the kingdom.

LAZARO. As if you can.

BUSTAMANTE. The *carteles* put a price on his head. With him gone, you are your own man. Everything is yours. The plant, the house, finances, this whore, *todo.* Grant my cargo passage. Leave the rest to me.

LAZARO. He is my father.

(**BUSTAMANTE** *takes a packet and slits it open.* **LAZARO** *takes a nailful of powder and runs it along his gum. A recognition.*)

BUSTAMANTE. Do you know this, Robles? Do you remember?

LAZARO. T-rex.

BUSTAMANTE. He raised you on this.

LAZARO. When do we start.

BUSTAMANTE. I'll let you know. Leave your cell phone on.

(*She goes.*)

SONIA. I AM NOT A WHORE, *PUTA!*

(*Lights change.* **PEPÍN** *hobbles in. He is severely beaten.*)

PEPÍN. *Va ver pedo.* Gonna be some big gas trouble. Cause a me telling the *Big Queso* everything. My sister *es mi brotha,* my mama is mama is midwife *tambien* to the baby I seen. And how we come lookin' for the lost *Sincero,* I told him! How in my sleepies I see *Dreamlandia* calling all of us home.

(**FRANK** *enters, in another area.*)

FRANK. This theme park, this Mexico, *circo de* hell. Goddamn Lazaro was right. I go the vertigo. Everywhere I turn I see my girl, And Dolores a thousand times over nailin' me with her looks. *¡Yo estar mucho borracho!*

PEPÍN. I know! I'll call my *San Francisco!*

(**PEPÍN** *takes out the ear, keys into it like a cell-phone.*)

Pi pa pi pa pa pa pi.

FRANK. The world's gone tequila, Tino! I hope that poor boy eviscerates you!…

(**PEPÍN** *calls into the ear.*)

PEPÍN. Hallooo!

(**FRANK** *reacts.*)

FRANK. OW!

PEPÍN. Halloo!

FRANK. What the….?

PEPÍN. Knock knock.

FRANK. Who's there?

PEPÍN. Cara…

FRANK. Cara who?

PEPÍN. Cara lotta wax in this thing, *vato*!

(**PEPÍN** *shoves his finger in.* **FRANK** *writhes in pain.*)

FRANK. AAARGH!

PEPÍN. There. Better. Reception clear!

FRANK. I'm losin' it! Holy God!

PEPÍN. Ain't no god here. Only *San Pedo*, the patron saint of human *piñatas* and porky rinds from heaven! Say *Amen*!

FRANK. I'm losing my fuckin' wits!

(**FRANK** *starts to go but* **PEPÍN**'s *voice yanks him back.*)

PEPÍN. Get your honky butt back, *jefe*! I told yoos to say amen!

FRANK. AMEN!

PEPÍN. That's more like it.

FRANK. I see how it is. Them people, the poor wet-backs that I wet back to die, they're angels, right! Yer an *angelito*! Alla heaven is a holding pen fulla Mexicans! Lined up in Judgment! The Lord *habla Español*!

PEPÍN. That's right.

FRANK. Only manly thing to do.

PEPÍN. What?

FRANK. Mosey across *La Avenida de las Americas*. Step in front of a big rig.

PEPÍN. *Pero por* why?

FRANK. I can't live with this.

PEPÍN. Hell, we do!

FRANK. You don't unnerstand. Here's where I drove my own bloodkin. I see them everywhere. A common girl in a factory turns into my daughter! I see my woman in the faces of the poor! I can't take it!

(*FRANK takes a step. The honks and screeches of cars.*)

PEPÍN. BUT SHE NEEDS YOU, SINCERO!

(*FRANK steps back.*)

FRANK. What...who, who needs me?

PEPÍN. *Lo sabes bien, Papo.*

FRANK. Blanca.

PEPÍN. I had a dream. With all of us in it. *Duermevato,* you, me, Blanca and Mami Dolores. I know the place. She's there for you. Follow the voice in your hole and I'll take you to her. Follow. Follow.

(*PEPÍN and FRANK go. Lights change. LAZARO and SONIA undressed in the hotel room. A bacchanalia of coke.*)

SONIA. Looka me! Looka Sonia del Valle now, motherfuckahs! She rams herself splat against the pane of three am and morning shatters to pieces at her feet of *puro* silk! She got a new body on, wider hips, glamor lips, fine lookin babe, feeling loosy goosy wearing danger like a fang! No more of that plant, trade my *maquila* for a shotta tequila, see ya girls, I'm done with your *chile, chiquitas*! And no more old man, taking his damn astrology charts to bed like they're gonna help! Ha! Miss Thing is leaving your moon, *viejo*.

LAZARO. Cover girl roar, cover girl hot!

SONIA. And to think I coulda been your mother! Vivian!

LAZARO. Wait. You knew her?

SONIA. One nasty cokehead, according to Tino. He couldn't let nobody know he was in deep with the cartels. So when time came for you to show your pretty head, he wouldn't take her to the hospital and –

LAZARO. She died giving *luz*.

SONIA. She was Frank's sister, too! Frank's your uncle! Junior, you're a therapist's goldmine!

LAZARO. I guess I am.

SONIA. Tell me again! When do we get rich?

LAZARO. Soon as Bustamante calls, I send my attorney to expose the shameful scandal of my father. The DEA find his ass to pay, hey, I'm a son of the USA, then its *tu y yo* in St Tropez.

SONIA. Wicked boy! How did you ever come up with this plot?

LAZARO. I read the synopsis in TV Guide.

(*She laughs. They kiss.* **CELESTINO**, **SETH**, *and* **CARL** *walk in.*)

SONIA. Shit.

CELESTINO. A long time ago, a *partera* told me that my wife would bear me a terrible son. That he would bring ruin on my head, usurp the love of my woman, and devour my life. Mandated by the stars, she said.

LAZARO. What took you so long?

SONIA. Celestino…I can explain….

CELESTINO. Please, Sonia, there is nothing to explain. You were the unfortunate wedge between fate and free will.

LAZARO. Do what you want with me. Just leave her alone.

SONIA. You…you knew he was coming?

CELESTINO. She made her choices.

LAZARO. And I made mine. But she has nothing to do with this. Let her go.

SONIA. Tino, you have to believe me –

CELESTINO. Quiet, Sonia.

LAZARO. You and me, *Papá.*

(**LAZARO** *'s cell phone rings.*)

CELESTINO. Go on. Pick it up.

(*As* **LAZARO** *reaches for the phone,* **CELESTINO** *slam his head to the table and knocks him out.* **SETH** *and* **CARL** *grab him as* **TINO** *answers the phone.*)

CELESTINO. Yes. Yes. Good.

(*He hangs up. As* **LAZARO** *is taken out,* **SONIA** *gathers her clothes.*)

SONIA. Tino, he he he coerced me, he got me high, he made made made me take it, I swear, I didn't I didn't I love you….

CELESTINO. Let's get us some air, *querida.* Go for a drive.

(*Lights change.*)

SONIA. Where are you taking me?

CELESTINO. *Mira.* Dots of dead ice. We study these sad flecks to understand how we started, to measure something of our future in them. We assign weight and substance to these insubstantial echoes of light. But if we're observing the light of stars long

ago put out, then what do *they* see, but the light of
our sun already millions of light years dead? What
does that make us? *¿Como damos luz?*

SONIA. I'm sorry. I was…overwhelmed.

CELESTINO. My wife died of this shit. It's an unpardon-
able practice.

SONIA. What are you going to do?

CELESTINO. I'm setting you free, Sonia. Go. Follow the
stars home, stay off the street. Some of my employ-
ees have met a rough end here.

(He goes.)

SONIA. CELESTINO! YOU CAN'T LEAVE ME HERE!
FOR THE LOVE OF GOD!

*(Shadowy PRESENCES gather around her, skulk-
ing.)*

Oh no…oh no…*señores…guapos…*please..

(They stand at a distance.)

SONIA. *(cont.)* They found her half-buried in the desert.

(They edge closer.)

Sonia with a new body. It was her scent that drew
them to her. Not Estee Lauder. Not Mirabella. Not
even Calvin Klein. The essence of Sonia. *Soñar. To
dream. Sueños sueños son.*

*(Darkness sweeps her up. Lights change. BLANCA
sits before the opened suitcase of her mother. DOLO-
RES enters.)*

DOLORES. *¿Que, mija?*

BLANCA. I was in him. Inside the man feeling his bones
and muscles, the gone-to-shit dreams of *gringo-*
hood, guiding me from one shore to the other.
The whole time I thought it was him.

DOLORES. It was you, *mija*. Always you.

BLANCA. I am my father's daughter.

DOLORES. But where was Sincero? Why was he deaf to me that night?

(**DOLORES** *holds up the coat and* **BLANCA** *places her arm through the sleeve. Her hand emerges from the cuff as Frank's and it gently touches* **DOLORES**' *face.*)

BLANCA. I was there. On the levee. Hiding from myself.

DOLORES. Sincero…

BLANCA. All my bones turned to shame.

DOLORES. Why didn't you come?

BLANCA. I couldn't. He woulda killed you. He woulda shot you in the water if I tried to save you.

DOLORES. Better dead than so unloved.

BLANCA. I loved you always, my love never failed you.

DOLORES. *You* did. Will you fail Blanca too?

BLANCA. My girl. Pretty, bold and true as her mother. I wish I'd known her.

DOLORES. Do you?

BLANCA. I'm sorry for lots of things in my life, but not her.

(**DOLORES** *kisses her hand as it slips back into the sleeve and* **BLANCA** *removes the coat.*)

That was him that spoke, Ama, but it was me, too.

DOLORES. *(taking one of the jars from the case)* For you, I've made a special tea. How much you drink will kill you, steal your wits, or make you face the devil.

(**BLANCA** *drinks. Gags. Feels herself change. Then she turns toward the river with resolve.*)

BLANCA. I was born here, but decided there. It's there I have to go.

(**BLANCA** *closes the case, and charges with it into the water. Thunder. Lights change. The island.*

CELESTINO *surveys the skies as* SETH *and* CARL *carry* LAZARO *on in his old rags. They shackle him to his chain.)*

SETH. Hurry. He's wakin' up, Carl.

LAZARO. *Ay.....*

CARL. Hey, pilgrim....

LAZARO. Sonia?

CARL. No, buddy. It's me. How you feelin'?

(thunder overhead)

CELESTINO. *Desmadre* is the forecast in the skies tonight.

LAZARO. Where am I?

CELESTINO. I feel it. The constellations crashing to earth.

LAZARO. Oh no...

CELESTINO. Bearing down like gods toward the border.

LAZARO. Not again.

CARL. It was all a bad dream, Laz. You been passed out since you drank this Extra-strength T-rex-inna-thermos, remember? Remember?

LAZARO. *¿Solo un sueño?*

CELESTINO. *Igual como la vida, hijo.*

SETH. It must've been a good dream, chief. I hope you got laid.

(A storm commences with loud claps of thunder and lightning.)

LAZARO. As if *que si.* As if *que no.* As if this life dreamt that life which dreamt this and which is real and which is just wish, wish, wish them back, no fuck that! No way no way NO WAY!

CELESTINO. Consider it a dream. It was too short, too violent, too senseless to have been anything else. This is the only world you know.

LAZARO. I was Lazaro Robles.

CELESTINO. And I was your father. But we all gotta wake up some time.

(SETH and CARL draw their weapons.)

LAZARO. What…what are you doing?

CELESTINO. One final piece of business. Doña Bustamante designated this checkpoint for her shipment. Your *isla* is our beach head.

SETH. There! I see something there!

CELESTINO. Do you hear me, *vieja*! I'm ready!

(They sees BLANCA rise out of the water toward him.)

You.

LAZARO. Cover girl.

BLANCA. I said I'd come back to free you.

CELESTINO. What are you doing here?

BLANCA. I am your *contrabanda*, Celestino.

Distilled by time and my mother's tears, the last narcotic to cross your *frontera*. The years you barricaded yourself with an empire of shit. Look at him! He's your son! No-one caused her to die but you, you proud sick *pendejo*. Hear your woman's truth as my mother sealed it in a jar –

(She opens a jar and a long cry sails over them. SETH and CARL cower in fear. She then takes the ropes from the case.)

Remember these? These cords bear witness, these ropes know what he's owed, not just in light, breath, blood, and time, but in Love. LOVE.

CELESTINO. No.

BLANCA. The key.

(SETH gives her the key and she advances toward LAZARO. CELESTINO aims the gun.)

One kilo of the truth, *patron*. Tell your son why his mother died.

(She waits for a moment, then unshackles him.)

LAZARO. Tell me, Apa.

CELESTINO. It was not my fault. It was hers. Dolores. *Curandera maldita,* you set the stars against me.

(loud clap of thunder)

Mojada, you're dead! *Una sombra!* As *if que si!* As if *que la chingada!* I make the border! I make the countries! I make the chain! I am *el mero* skin of God, *puta!*

CARL. Put the gun down, Mr. Robles.

CELESTINO. *¡Mira! Espantos, fantasmas,* wading in the *rio.* Crying for the homeblood. The blood is *voz.* The *voz* has mouth. Mouth has wound. Wound is...

(He fires. A shrill piercing cry merges with thunder.)

FRANK. *(off)* Don't shoot! Hold yer damn fire! God-dammit! GODDAM-ALMIGHTY!

SETH. That's the chief!

(FRANK *lurches on with the limp bleeding body of* **PEPÍN.** *)*

BLANCA. PEPÍN!

FRANK. Lookit what you done! Bastards! Lookit what you done to my SON!

CELESTINO. Did you see her, Frank? Your woman's out on the water again!

FRANK. You're all right, boy. You'll be fine.

PEPÍN. Blanca, you're back. *Hola,* Thirst. don't need googles nomore.

SETH. We gotta get you a doctor, little guy.

FRANK. Go! Now!

(SETH and CARL run off.)

BLANCA. Oh my god, Pepín! You're bleeding!

FRANK. I'm sorry! I tried not to let this happen! But he said to come because there was this –

PEPÍN. *¡Alli!* I see it! LOOK!

(He breaks away and wraps his eyes around his vision.)

Mi gran sueño! The dream that dreamed me first. Look through the hole in my chest at the gold of *Dreamlandia, vatos.*

(As they begin to move toward a threshold, the lights change and the storm abates, and they see what **PEPÍN** *sees.)*

Ghostcrossers in a Spanish play played many nights before, before the before. Strangers passing through each others' *corazones.* I see them. A King. A Prince. A Royal Lady. An old Duke. But where's the Fool? Gotta have a Fool.

(As they move slowly through another space, they step toward each other.)

Ahh. Now I see these shadows tip heaven on its side, not the other way around.

*(***CELESTINO*** *faces* **LAZARO***;* **BLANCA** *faces* **FRANK.***)*

CELESTINO. If stars keep their word, then so must I; do with me what you will.

LAZARO. There was no verdict but that you passed on yourself. *Señor, levanta, dame tu mano.*

*(***LAZARO*** *takes his hand.)*

FRANK. You are my daughter and that's enough to live for.

BLANCA. My mother was good; she deserved a better death.

FRANK. I'll honor her with my own for your sake.

BLANCA. *Padre, me daz luz otra vez.*

(He kisses her hand.)

PEPÍN. *Suave. Pero* where's the Fool? *Yo no veo el* Fool.

LAZARO. *(to* **FRANK** *and* **BLANCA***)* To you both I grant all the mercy you desire. To my father, forgiveness.

BLANCA. This is it.

CELESTINO. This is how we conquer fate.

FRANK. In story. Old dramas long ago played out.

(**PEPÍN** *dies. The lights change back. The sound of a light rain on the water. They seem to wake from the dream. Embarrassment and helplessness.)*

BLANCA. Can't we pretend, can't we make everything from before...

FRANK. No.

CELESTINO. No.

LAZARO. ...No.

(She goes to **PEPÍN***.)*

BLANCA. He's dead. *(weeping over his broken body)* How do we wake up from this dream, this nightmare?

FRANK. Maybe we don't.

CELESTINO. Maybe he just did.

(**LAZARO** *takes to the shackle and holds it up to* **CELESTINO***.)*

LAZARO. Why did you let her die?

(**CELESTINO** *takes it, feels the weight of the chain in his hands, and then slowly brings the shackle up to* **LAZARO***'s face.)*

CELESTINO. To save you.

(**CELESTINO** *drops the shackle and creeps into* **LAZARO***'s hovel.)*

LAZARO. *Si asi es, asi es.*

BLANCA. Apa.

FRANK. I can't be your father. I don't know how. I don't...

(**DOLORES** *appears as a faint image over water.)*

DOLORES. Sincero.

FRANK. Dolores?

BLANCA. It's her.

DOLORES. *¡Sincero!*

FRANK. Over here! Dolores, I got our boy!

DOLORES. *Cuidado, mi amor.* It's deep and cold.

FRANK. *(taking* **PEPÍN** *in his arms)* I ain't afraid. I'm comin'. *(turning to* **BLANCA***)* I wish in some world we coulda been...well...

DOLORES. *Yo he sufrido tanto por tu ausencia*
Desde ese dia hasta hoy, no soy feliz —

(**FRANK** *wades with* **PEPÍN** *into the river toward* **DOLORES.***)*

FRANK. I'm comin', Dolores, I'm comin'...

(They vanish in the current.)

BLANCA. It's over, cuz.

LAZARO. You and me. *¿Somos familia?*

BLANCA. All that's left of it.

LAZARO. And Alfonso?

BLANCA. He's still around.

LAZARO. We better go before one of us wakes up. But where? Which side?

(**BLANCA** *takes his hand and slowly guides him into the water with her. Step by step.)*

BLANCA. We just go, Lazaro, *tu y yo*, we step into the flux of our world, this river, we go in, eyes opened, hearts bent toward the land that needs us most; we go in breathing and let the water decide.

(They walk the water and exit. **CELESTINO** *alone. Blackout.)*

End Play

Also by
Octavio Solis...

Lydia

Bethlehem

Please visit our website **samuelfrench.com** for complete
descriptions and licensing information.

9 780573 697999